Smoke

HEARTS AND ASHES
BOOK ONE

IRISH WINTERS

COPYRIGHT

Smoke, Hearts and Ashes, Book 1

Cover design by Letitia Hasser, Romantic Book Designs, http://www.rbadesigns.com
Interior book design by Bob Houston eBook Formatting

ISBN Paperback: 978-1-942895-82-4
ISBN eBook: 978-1-942895-60-2

Irish Winter's author websites are:
http://www.irishwinters.com and irishwinters.blogspot.com

DEDICATION

Not all who wander are lost...
J. R. R. Tolkien

You can find Irish Winters on Facebook:
https://www.facebook.com/author.irishwinters

On Twitter:
https://twitter.com/irishwinters1

For news on upcoming releases, sign up
for Irish Winters' Newsletter at
IrishWinters.com/Newsletter.

For more information about all my
books, visit IrishWinters.com.

PROLOGUE

"You shoulda been there," Clem Hardy drawled, his voice edged with anger.

Just frickin' great. Smoke stopped walking. Calls from his home state were never good news, less so when delivered by crotchety older men, who thought they knew everything just because they lived next door—in Texas—oh, by the way.

Humping through the western jungle of Vietnam, the ex-Navy SEAL had been headed back to Cambodia, the place Smoke called home the past couple years, until his sat phone buzzed an incoming. But now? Who knew where the hell he'd be going.

The sun had just risen east of the Mekong. Birds were up and squawking their beaks off, and for once, he felt good. The jungle didn't yet stifle, because the sun wasn't high enough. Walking was easy. He knew where he was going because he knew where he'd been. He'd followed his gut and did what he'd wanted. He'd met his hero, Tucker Chase, another SEAL. Everything was good—until Clem called.

Smoke got right to the point. "What now?"

"A little thing called an F5, you ungrateful punk," Clem bit out.

"Now Father, don't get riled at the boy before he knows what happened," Betty sputtered. "For crying out loud, your blood pressure's climbing through the roof. You know better."

Smoke bit his tongue, fighting for calm. If he lived to be a hundred, he'd never understand why some wives called their husbands, *Father*. It smacked of too much female submission for him, another thing he never understood. Women were equally as strong as men. They fought as hard, marched as long, and they mourned for their fallen companions as deeply. Maybe deeper. Why settle for less?

He raked a hand through his too-long-for-Navy, jet black hair. "When?" he asked, needing this call to be short. It had already missed the sweet marker.

"Two guldurned nights ago is when!" Clem shouted over the nearly nine thousand miles between them. "It's gone! The whole damned thing's gone! You shoulda been here, not gallivanting all over the world!"

"Now Father, don't go scaring the boy like that. It's not all gone. Just our barn's gone and…" The connection rattled. Betty must've grabbed the phone or Clem dropped it since she took over telling the bad news. "Smoke? Are you there? Can you hear me, boy?"

It never got better than being called *boy* after all a man did for his country. Smoke gave up counting to ten. There weren't enough numbers in the universe to squelch the angst in his gut, so he pushed his opinion of home-sweet-home down deep and low. Saved it for later. But what was gone? Clem's barn or—?

"I'm here," he answered, toeing the tangled root in his path. Betty wasn't so bad. She'd be better if she left her old man, though. Maybe then she wouldn't have to sneak the moonshine she kept hidden in the weeds behind her chicken coop. Hell, maybe then she wouldn't need booze at all.

Clem railed in the background. "They needed you, boy, but where in Sam hill were ya! Sure as hell not where you shoulda been!"

Smoke's gut pitched acid. *They* needed him? As in—*them?*

Betty talked louder and faster, no doubt because Clem was prowling and grumbling behind her. "A powerful tornado touched down outside of Garland, that's what Clem's trying to tell you. We thought we were going to be safe, but you know how those storms are. The funnel skipped over the mall. It barely did any damage, but then it tucked tail and headed our way. It hit us hard, boy. We lost our barn and silo. Most of our cattle run off or got sucked up into the vortex." She coughed. "We ain't found 'em yet, but I swear, it was like God pointed his finger at your folks and us. The neighbor on the other side lost a few trees and everything at your folks' place isn't gone. It's mostly still there, the stable and the house. The funnel only grabbed some trees and..." She coughed again. "It took... th-th-them."

She started bawling and sniffling, while Smoke tried to feel anything for the far-off parents he'd barely spoken with in years. He and his old man never got along. Same kind of bastards and all that rot. Which was why he didn't go home to Texas after the Navy. Fundamentally at odds with his parents, he'd been exiled the day he took up the trident and promised fealty to his country. Smoke wouldn't apologize for that, and his dad wouldn't have listened if he did.

Why Vietnam and Cambodia? Why Southeast Asia? Simple. Smoke hadn't been there before. He wanted to see the world. There was no place else to go. Hell, just because the grass was greener. In other words, when a man didn't want to do something, any excuse worked.

Rolling the strangling knot of tension out of his neck, he wished he felt something more than regret. It'd been a long time since he'd thought of home.

"Can you hear me, darlin'? Are you still there, boy?" It sounded like Betty thumped her phone on the counter.

God, don't call me darlin'. Or boy.

"Yes, ma'am. I'm still here," Smoke replied as he looked east to the golden light filtering through the brush and elephant grass. Mornings brought peace to his soul. He didn't know why, only knew he liked himself better at sunrise, at the start of a new day. Funny though. By the time the dark rolled around again, the peaceful feeling always fled. Every day ended in the same foul frame of mind. Wishing he'd died in combat, so the battles replaying in his head would cease. So, his optimistic brain wouldn't begin misleading him the next day to believe things could get better. They couldn't. He'd long since traded optimism for reality.

"Sure sorry to hafta notify you like this," Betty mumbled.

"Thanks for calling," Smoke offered for lack of anything better to say.

"We'd be pleased if you'd consider staying with us when you come home, son."

"I thought you said the tornado took them?"

"Well, it didn't exactly *take them*, take them. It just kinda killed them. There still needs to be a funeral. You're coming home for that, aren't you?"

He honestly didn't know. It seemed a long way to go to plant two people who'd chosen not to speak to him, the not-so-loving or forgiving mother and father who'd returned his letters even while he was in far off combat zones. Who'd disowned and denied they'd had a son, all because he'd expressed a deep-seated desire to serve his country. Of course, then he'd made it worse by voting for the wrong president. Then he became a SEAL, what his liberal father termed assassins and a mercenary. Smoke wasn't sure who were the bigger bastards, the men who fought for their country or the cowards who wouldn't.

Yet his father had lived his life under the same flag Smoke had damned near given his all for. So yeah. Texas was a helluva long way to go to relive two of his worst memories, disrespect from his old man's know-it-all neighbor and losing—her.

"Come on, son, friends and family will be stopping by. Everyone wants to see you. They do." Betty sounded sad but hopeful. "The pastor'll be by and the mayor. Folks are asking about you."

I doubt that.

Smoke stalled. The child within had always nagged to go home. It urged him now to at least, see his mother and father before they were buried. To tell them goodbye.

His heart softened. There was a time they'd loved him. They'd both told him so. Then. And he wasn't the one who'd disowned them. He'd never stopped loving them, either. He'd just spent a long time wishing things would've been different, that he could've changed things with his father. That stubborn old man was the crux of the problem. If Caleb had changed, Caroline would've followed his lead.

"There's gonna be a real nice service," Betty coaxed. "Please come home, Smoke. I know your father wasn't an easy man to live with, but your mama missed you. You know she did."

He shook his head, not responding out loud. If Mom loved him, she never told him after he'd been sent packing. Not after his father declared him dead. Smoke never understood Caroline choosing loyalty to Caleb over the love of her only child.

He closed his eyes and wished he hadn't answered his phone. Not exactly true. He wouldn't have carried the damned thing if he hadn't hoped that someday, somehow...

Ah, bullshit. Screw that fairytale. He carried it to keep in touch with the real world, and for the last years, that world had had nothing to do with Texas.

"I'll make up the guest room at my place, so you don't have to—"

"No." He didn't mean to bark that word, but hell no. He wouldn't stay under the same roof as his father's adversary. Clem Hardy was ten times the pessimistic man Smoke had become. "Thanks for the offer, but I'll stay at my folks' place if I come back," he clarified, softening his tone. *If I come back. I'm still not decided.*

"It's your place now, son," she murmured.

Shit. He hadn't thought of that. Or that he was his parent's only heir. Everything they owned was now his. *Damn.* Their ranch. Their horses. *Double damn.* The oil rig on the lower forty. There'd be a lawyer involved and a will. There'd be legalities and probate. There'd be talk behind his back in town, and he'd have to stay in Texas longer than a few days. He'd have to sell the ranch, and that meant...

Son-of-a-bitch. His chest heaved at the thought of returning home to the land that he loved. A familiar sensation sprang to life, one he'd fought to control too many times in the middle of dark, quiet nights. America never was the problem. *The Lost Chaparral* was.

"I'll be there." Smoke signed off before Betty could get out another sniffle. Stuffing the phone in its holster, he glared at the lush jungle before him, not seeing anything. Only the stern proud face of his father, his black brows scowling over eyes as fierce and as passionate as Smoke's. The beautiful smile of his mother, the woman who should've stood up to Caleb Montoya and defended her son. Who should've had his back but didn't.

Dragging the phone back up, he thumbed another number.

She answered. His buddy. His roommate. The one he trusted. Colby Quaid.

"I'm not making it in tonight. I'm going to Texas," he bit out, letting his annoyance show.

"So? Why you calling me?"

"Didn't want you to worry. This might take a while."

"I never worry about you. Ride easy. Sleep hard."

She hung up before he could explain further. That was Colby for you. Rough and tumble. Over-confident. Former Army Sergeant Colby Quaid.

Smoke growled at the monkeys chattering overhead.

Damn it. I'm going home.

CHAPTER ONE

Tornado alley. The region in North America prone to the most lethal tornadoes. Texas. Oklahoma. North to Canada. Sometimes as far south as Alabama. Dallas-Fort Worth had seen its share of F5s and their wickedly unpredictable baby brothers. All powerful reminders of what ruled this planet, and it wasn't mankind.

Smoke endured the bumpy ride into DFW International Airport. Inclement weather, nothing. The aircraft pitched and yawed its descent through angry black thunderheads and sheeting rain. At last it touched down onto the slick runway with a sideways shift through capricious wind sheer and window-cracking hail. It seemed not even the Texas skies were happy to see him. Helluva welcome home.

Inclement weather posed brain-splitting headaches and hostile, stranded passengers for the airline staff. Smoke wanted nothing to do with that drama. Grabbing his duffle bag with his few newly purchased personal items he'd picked up in Hồ Chí Minh City prior to the flight, he ducked into his preordered rental car at the curb and left hectic DFW behind.

Interstate 30 took him northeast of Sunnyvale to *The Lost Chaparral*. Sunday traffic was light. Smoke rolled the windows down and popped the sunroof on his rental for a deep breath of late springtime on the prairie. A few yellow creosote blossoms still lingered along the roadsides. The wild mesquite scrub brush hadn't turned dry and brown yet. Even the buffalo grass growing knee-high in the ditches was blue-green at this gentle time of year.

This was his corner of Texas, the Blackland Prairies. Over twelve million acres of grass, it boasted a rolling scene of oak, elm and pecan, a horde of invasive flowering pear and Russian Olive, as well as plenty of thistle and creeping briar. He only knew the names because his mother did. At least she used to.

Drumming his fingers on the steering wheel, Smoke remembered better days. His parents hadn't always hated him.

At the interstate exit, he turned south. By the time he arrived at the ranch, the wind had died down, the storm was spent, and the sun came out. Smoke tugged his Oakleys out of his shirt pocket to shield his eyes. It wasn't until he caught sight of the two mighty log uprights and the oxen hitch sign that proudly proclaimed *Lost Chaparral* hanging between them that he saw the wicked path left by the F5.

He swallowed hard past the knot in his throat and the thump in his heart, unprepared for the destruction before him. Until now, the drive had been pleasant. But now...

Smoke hit the brakes. He'd expected bad, but this was—worse. Other than Clem's place, no other neighbors had sustained much damage. This was a surgical strike. Real finger of God devastation.

Parking behind a dusty Chevy pickup he didn't recognize, Smoke climbed out of his ride for a better look. Damn. The Hardy's pole barn two miles west of his parents' ranch had been wiped from the earth, leaving nothing but shards of lumber and eight-by-eights scattered across their pasture. The red asphalt shingles on their roof were gone, the plywood stripped, the joists bare. The oddest sight though, a black Cadillac, rested nose down in the field behind their house, its door splayed open like a big, dead bug's wings. Tornadoes did the weirdest things, but that took the cake.

The Lost Chaparral? Eerily quiet. Smoke drew in a long, slow breath and blew it out just as slowly. The house still stood. The stable and barn appeared untouched, but no chickens pecked for bugs and grasshoppers on the front lawn. No patient horses stood saddled at the front door hitch, nickering to him for an apple or a scratch behind their ears.

Giant live oaks had once lined the brick drive. Over the years, they'd created a tunnel of shade and memories, of Smoke learning to ride his first bike, and skinning his knees when he fell. Of racing Jasper or Minks, his old man's mules, home for dinner with a fast clip and boyish enthusiasm, calling for his mother to *'Quick. Come see!'* Of carving a heart into the bark of one of those trees for a special girl who'd had better things to do than to fall for him.

Yeah. Good times.

Then.

The century-old trees now lay scattered like toys across the expansive front lawn, as if some giant child had tossed them aside after rough and rowdy play. Rain-filled craters and gullies pockmarked where the trees' massive taproots had stretched deep into the fertile prairie. The spotty path of the capricious F5 was clear and telling. Its debris field stretched from the ditch opposite the road in front of the ranch and straight up *Lost Chaparral's* drive. A tractor rested on upside down in the field across the road. Might be Clem's. Didn't look like one of Caleb's, not that Smoke knew what equipment his old man used anymore. But the giant oak, stripped of leaves and laying on its side where Hardy's barn once stood, that was definitely Caleb Montoya's. Clem must really hate that.

There was so much destruction in so little distance. So. Damned. Much. But there it stopped, at the front porch of the Montoya hacienda like an Amway salesman who'd been sent packing. As if Gandalf himself had bellowed, *'You shall not pass!'*

Nothing else appeared damaged. The house was still standing. The semi-circle of sentinel oaks behind the clay-tiled home still stood guard. His mother's brightly colored Talavera pots still graced the brick steps at the front porch as if nothing as wicked as an F5 had touched down. Even the red-washed stables and barn in the field seemed untouched.

Just not the gentle giants that had guarded *The Lost Chaparral.*

Just not the red brick drive.

Just not—*Mom and Dad.*

Which made no sense. Why weren't they in the storm cellar? That was the hard-fast rule. Caleb Montoya had drilled tornado safety into his son's head over the years. Why hadn't the proud man followed his own damned advice? Was he arrogant enough to think a tornado wouldn't touch him? That would've been just like Caleb to think he was invincible.

For the first time in years, a tear eked out of the corner of Smoke's eye. Like them or not, respect what they'd done to him or not, he had loved his parents. And he knew it.

"Goddamnit," breathed out of him in a ragged sigh. He walked into the disaster zone, his mind in a daze, a tremendously huge part of him unable to grasp the obvious fact that his prior life and his parents were gone. The trees lay in his way. Some nosy neighbor had tacked a flyer on the first downed oak, the one blocking the drive with its massive trunk. Angling his wide shoulders between the leafless branches, he ripped the message from the scarred tree trunk that, even on its side, dwarfed him by a good three feet. Whoever'd left It must've been one determined son-of-a-bitch.

Smoke wiped a hand over his hair, thinking someone cared enough to have left a kind word. Wrong again.

Looking for easy? So am I!
Jenkins Lassiter Real Estate will gladly buy your
disaster-plagued property
Today!
No questions asked!
No disaster too big!
Let us turn your misfortune into the first Sunnyvale
Casino
Complete with swimming pool, 18-hole golf course, and
RV Park!
Limited time offer.
Don't miss your chance!

Bullshit. Crumpling the flyer, Smoke tossed it away from the dying tree. Who the hell was Jenkins

Lassiter, an over-the-top attention grabber? *Dumbass.*

With one hand pressed to the bark, Smoke's chin dropped to his chest and his gut clenched tight at the loss of—everything. The life and history of *The Lost Chaparral* had been cruelly ripped out of his hands and tossed to the sky, its remnants reduced to a quick sale at the hands of a money-grubbing nobody.

A growling sob caught in his throat, choking Smoke with regret. Unprepared for the violent grief clawing its way out of him, the anger of an unloved and unwanted son roared to life, lashing back at the two people who should've cared for him, but who were no longer within reach. An orphaned child sprang to life in his soul, only to drown in the remorse and lost opportunities that could never come again. The wish for a father's forgiveness that wouldn't be asked for, nor extended. The desperate craving for a mother's gentle touch. The bitter taste of '*if only.*' The story of his life. But remorseful '*whys*' weren't meant to be answered, were they? Smoke already knew the answer—heavenly silence.

It took less than a moment to grapple with his demons. A man couldn't exactly forsake the home he hadn't been welcome in. Neither could he change the past, nor relinquish his honor to please others. Not even angry parents. No. Smoke hadn't deserted his post in this family. Caleb and Caroline had done that to him. Here in the great state of Texas, where guns were a way of life for most folks, his pacifist father was the exception to the rule.

But that was yesterday...

Sucking in a deep breath, Smoke let the ghosts of his past go. Shoving his way out of the ragged, tattered embrace of the dying oak, he returned to his rental, grabbed his duffle bag out through the open window, and left the vehicle locked on the road where he'd parked it. He had work to do.

Those downed trees needed to be gone, their massive bulks hauled away to some lumber yard, and new trees planted in their place. This ranch, with its southwestern design and cowboy flair, hadn't been his home for years. It wouldn't be hard to let it go, and he meant to offer it at one helluva discount, not to Jenkins Lassiter Real Estate though. The thought of a casino sprawled over these wild prairies seemed wrong.

Slinging his bag over his shoulder, Smoke placed one hand to the trunk of the first tree and vaulted over it. At every turn, the single-mindedness of this family tragedy galled him. It truly looked as if that devil-twister had held a grudge against *The Lost Chaparral.* It not only downed the trees that lined the red brick driveway but stripped the bricks themselves as if it couldn't tolerate a hint of Montoya welcome. Long muddy ruts now pointed the way to the hacienda like evil, bony fingers. The home itself stood untouched, but the brick drive was gone. Erased. The twister had scrubbed it bare, yet no tiles from the hacienda roof were missing. *How odd.*

His mother's cheery geraniums still bloomed at each side of the three-step brick porch, as if nothing so bizarre as a wicked F5 had struck just feet from them. The porch looked as if she might step out the front door to water her flowers any minute now. Even his father's cowboy boots were in their place, proud and dusty in the boot tray outside the door. As if he were still inside.

Despite the foolish hope climbing up his throat, Smoke faced the truth. Tornadoes did the damnedest things. Like that Cadillac stuck nose down in Clem's field, they picked and chose who to torment, who to let live, and who to kill. What to wipe from the face of the earth. What to leave untouched and unscathed. The phenomenon of

Mother Nature's force was not unexpected. Just hard to swallow.

Deliberately, he set his boots to each and every step, hesitating at the onslaught of memories of better times. He'd helped Caleb construct this porch when he was eight. It was a weeklong labor of love that had left Smoke feeling like a man for the first time in his life. Then...

Smoke paused at the door. He was the prodigal son, remember? He didn't have a key. Turned out he didn't need one. The wrought iron latch lifted easily at his fingertips. Why wouldn't it? Mom and Dad hadn't expected a tornado when they'd left the house that morning. No one had.

He swallowed hard and put his palm to the door, easing it inward. The last battle between him and his dad still lingered in the godawful silence within. All those ugly words spoken in haste reached out to him. They were still there. Every last one of them. Lurking.

Smoke took a deep breath, and with that final step...

He was home.

CHAPTER TWO

Jessie West, the face cameras loved, the legs other models wished they had, and the temperamental diva the paparazzi tormented every chance they got. Missing from the swimsuit photo shoot in Cannes, France. Or so the major fashion headlines declared. Like they knew anything about her.

Instead, she'd flown home for her brother's funeral disguised as her assistant, Barbara Esposito, in a private charter. If the press caught word of the trip, the story was that Barbara had taken Fluffy, Jessie's standard poodle, to Texas, in advance of her arrival. By the time, L'Officiel, Vogue, and Elle realized they'd been duped, she planned to be done with her goodbyes and back in the Big Apple.

By the time she'd hailed a cab at DFW to take her and Fluffy to the funeral parlor, then twenty-five miles to the West Ranch, her nails were chewed to the quick and the last of her make-up had been cried off. She'd flushed her extra-long, fluttery lashes down the toilet at the funeral parlor when she'd stopped for one last visit. Her heart was as raw as it had never been, even when she'd lost her parents.

Staring out the window with her faithful companion at her side, her heart gave way. Ethan, her older and only brother, her only true friend and her the last member of her family, was gone. The corny guy who'd always believed in her. Encouraged her. Pulled her hair and teased her. Made her believe she could fly. How could this nightmare have happened? Was any of this real?

The bitter irony of her presence—now when it was too late— was that Ethan had been right. He'd always believed, always told her she could fly. She'd not only flown, she'd soared. In less than a year, she'd become New York's favorite flavor. Her agent, Fernando Sonoma, *so not his real name,* knew all the right people. He'd kick-started her modeling career, and he was worth every penny Ethan paid the high-priced con artist.

That was precisely what Sonoma was, a one-click wheeler-dealer. If he couldn't get you into the industry, nobody could. But big brother Ethan had always told Jessie if she was going to make it, she'd have to pay for it. Only Ethan was the one who'd paid. He'd never stopped footing the exorbitant bills for the over-priced flesh peddler, even after her meteoric rise to fame, fortune, and success. He'd always believed in her, never doubted, even when she'd been too busy to come home last Christmas. When contracts and golden opportunities came up that interfered with the occasional reunion with her only sibling.

Damn it. The numbing loss hurt. This past year had gone by too quickly. Out of sheer arrogance and her over-the-top schedule, she'd lost touch with Ethan, and now she had to face the truth. There were no second chances. All the golden opportunities in the world couldn't bring back what she'd foolishly turned her back on. Death had come and it had ruthlessly tossed every last *round tuit* to the wind. An F5 wind.

Jessie shivered. She deserved this for not taking better care of her only sibling. For not being a decent sister. Regret kicked in again, crawling up her throat. Shoving her fist to her mouth, she muffled the scream in her heart. Fluffy whined, his paw on her shoulder in his cute, anxious way. She wiped her tender nose and stared out the window as the prairie she used to love with all her heart passed by.

Poor, poor Ethan.

The one thing Smoke and his old man had agreed on was horses. At one time, Caleb owned five of them, and Smoke honestly didn't know if he'd kept them and the two mules. After dropping his bag alongside the rose flowered couch in his mother's tidy front room, Smoke checked the landline. When a dial tone answered, he replaced the receiver and headed down the hall through the family-sized kitchen, the adjoining mudroom, and out the back door where the view was better.

There were still trees there. Their shade offered an odd sense of normalcy in the middle of the overwhelming grief sneaking up on him. He took a deep breath and shook it off. Unless the mules and horses had run off during the twister, they'd be in the back corral. It looked untouched. Could they have survived what humans hadn't?

"Hey, Smoke," a laid-back throaty voice murmured. "Good to see you, son."

Smoke startled as his dad's ranch hand, Jared Powers, rounded the stable.

The silver-haired guy had to be close to his seventies. Even his impressive handlebar mustache had turned white. Jared was a Sam Elliot look-alike if ever there was one, right down to his dusty jeans and boots. The cowboy hat pushed back on his silver hair made the resemblance even more so. Twice as laid back. Twice as set in his ways. He stuck out a callused hand, then jerked Smoke in for a chest bumping, backslapping guy hug that lasted long enough for him to grumble, "Sure sorry you had to come home like this."

Smoke could've cried. This simple welcome from someone who really knew him was all he'd wanted, only he'd wanted it from his dad. Needing distance to maintain his composure, he stepped back and jerked his head toward Clem and Betty's. "Why didn't *you* call me? Why them?"

Jared shook his head. "You know Betty. She said she needed your number because she was sending a care package your way. I believed her until she showed up at the mortuary, bragging you were finally coming home. Damned know-it-all."

That explained a lot. Betty had no life. She'd always delighted in knowing the latest gossip. The latest tragedy. It was a sad commentary on her home situation that other people's misfortunes made her somebody.

"Where are the horses?"

A shadow drifted through the glimmer in Jared's eyes. "I was just checking them. They're in the stable. They get antsy when the wind kicks up, but they'll settle down. They'll be fine."

"Chip?"

A wink and a few steps around the stable to the corral and the question answered itself. Chip, his father's fudge-brown Appaloosa gelding, stood with his chest to the rails, his head high and his dark mane tossed, his wide nostrils flared as he tested the wind. Chip, as gentle as the day was long, so named because a young boy with stars in his eyes declared those brown spots on his white rump looked *'like chocolate chips, Daddy!'*

Smoke swallowed hard. He knew exactly when this handsome fellow had been born. He'd been there. He'd seen this sweet colt slip out of his mother's belly and land in the straw, all legs and wet velvet fur. Seventeen years go. The golden memory of a better day hurt. God, didn't everything?

Chip nickered. The mares joined him at the gate. All hand-gentled, they milled against the metal bars until Smoke lifted the chain and let himself inside.

Jared hooked a boot heel over the bottom rail and leaned both elbows to the fence. "They remember you."

The gelding certainly did. Chip crowded Smoke, bumping his nose to Smoke's shoulder like one of the guys asking, *'Where you been, man?'*

It felt like a welcome home. Smoke reached for this rowdy guy's ears and scratched behind them, then smoothed a palm along the underside of Chip's thick mane, stroking the sun-warmed neck of a long-lost friend. "How you doing, fella?"

Crowding closer, the horse snorted, and damned if he didn't hang his head over Smoke's shoulder, absorbing the rub and giving back a hug of his own. Smoke rested his head against the big guy's muscular neck. The darkness he'd dragged around with him lifted a little. For the first time in ages, he could breathe.

"I plan on hanging around," Jared offered quietly. "Figured you'll need help with the place and the horses. The mules."

Smoke nodded, one hand still on Chip's wide neck, one hand on the halter. "Thanks. I will."

The next question, the one he expected to hear plenty over the next few days. "You planning on staying or selling?"

He met his father's hired hand in the eye. "I'm selling. Are you interested?" Jared buying him out would make everything easier. Quicker.

A spark of censure shifted over Jared's weathered, suntanned face. "I would if I could, but no. This place is too big for an old guy like me. It needs a woman's touch and someone to love it. I hoped that'd be you and your lady friend if you've got one."

Smoke didn't take the bait that Jared had chummed the welcome-home-waters with. Less said was always more in his book. The fewer words spoken, the easier it'd be to leave. "Let me know what I owe you."

Those bushy eyebrows lifted. "For what? Being neighborly?"

That stung. "No, for the chores you've been doing since they... since it happened."

Jared shook his head in that older, wiser way guys his age had before they overwhelmed you with what bullshit wisdom they thought they knew. "You've got a lot to learn, son. Some things can't be bought, and they don't need to be paid for, neither. You might not be familiar with it where you come from, but it's a little thing called friendship." He thumbed his hat back off his forehead. "It's called loyalty. I've been your old man's friend for as long as I can remember. Take it or leave it."

"I'll take it." Smoke meant to do whatever was necessary to get out of the country. Jared might as well get that straight now. "You know a good lumber yard?"

"For what? Those live oaks you lost out front?"

"For salvage lumber," Smoke clarified. "I want them gone. Once that mess is cleaned up, I'll haul in asphalt to fix the driveway."

"That *mess* was your dad's pride and joy," Jared said evenly.

Smoke caught the drift. *Rein it in. Don't be so quick to get out of town that you make more enemies. Keep it real.* Only it was too damned real. Caleb Montoya was everywhere, only he wasn't.

"I've already called Smitty. He'll take the trees off your hands. You remember him, don't you?"

Smoke nodded. Smitty Ferguson owned the nearest lumber mill, Smitty and Sons. "Yeah, I remember. No questions asked?"

"He's willing to do what needs to be done, Smoke. You do know you're not the only one who lost someone in this storm, don't you? Your buddy down the road died the day after the twister. I imagine Jessie will be flying in today for Ethan's funeral."

Smoke cast his gaze across his father's field to the two-story, white clapboard house five to the east. "Ethan? What happened?"

Jared's hat shifted down over his forehead, shielding his eyes. "Hell, you know Ethan. He'd lost a tree—one damned tree—and just like you, he wanted it gone. The day after the storm, he didn't ask anyone for help, just pitched in with his chainsaw and turned the branches to kindling. But his saw couldn't handle the girth of the trunk, and the tree was still green, hard to cut with an ordinary blade. They found him on his back staring at the sun, the chainsaw still in his fist."

"He bled out?" Damn. What an awful way to go.

"The saw didn't get him. It. Was the tree when it settled into the waterlogged ground and rolled. Crushed him."

Smoke didn't know what to say in the face of so much tragedy. Tears bit at the corners of his eyes. He'd grown up with Ethan and his sister, Jess. They were the family he'd never had. How much more could he take?

Jared let him have it. "So, think about that when you're too proud to ask for help, and you're doing things by yourself. It don't hurt to ask friends and neighbors for a hand. That's what we're here for."

That and gossip.

Smoke nodded, not that he agreed with Jared, but because that was what guys who weren't ready to commit did. He smoothed a gentling a hand over Chip's long, muscular neck before he gave him a smack and left his four-legged friend behind. "You want a cup of coffee?"

"No, thanks. Already had my one-cup for the day," Jared grumbled, his boots kicking up pieces of gravel the twister had scattered everywhere. "I just came over to tell you Minks caught a chunk of something in the storm with those big donkey ears of his. Damned near sheared one of 'em off."

Smoke scanned the fields looking for the missing fellows. "Where are they?"

"You know how mules are. Once I loaded Minks, Jasper took to braying and kicking the rails like an idiot. I didn't need another injury on my hands, so I loaded him up, too. They're brothers. They were scared and needed to be together, so they're at my place. Didn't think you'd mind."

Smoke ran his fingers over his short-cropped hair. Brothers he could relate to. "You're sure I can't pay for the vet bill?"

Jared smacked the middle of Smoke's back hard enough to make it sting. "You just don't get it. We're all reeling from losing your mom and dad, son. From losing Ethan, too. There's no vet bill and there never will be. This ain't Afghanistan, damn it. Folks care about each other 'round here. Doc Murdock came by the night the twister blew through. He already stitched up that ornery mule, and I helped him. Now drop the bullshit before I kick your ass. I can still do that, you know."

Smoke let it go. He could also relate to ass kicking. Folding his arms on the top rail of the corral, he cast his stare out to the open prairie. "Which funeral parlor?"

"Purdy's," Jared replied somberly. "Hope you don't mind, but I already took some clothes over. Your dad's dress slacks and his white shirt. His bolo tie with the Texas star. Your mom's pretty blue dress. The one she wore to church. Miss Tanner said she'll take care of her socks and those other things ladies wear."

"She always liked her hair up," Smoke remembered, his voice soft and distant. She might not have liked him there at the end, but Caroline was still his mom. He wanted her to look her best.

"Miss Tanner'll take care of that. Don't worry, they'll look..." Jared grunted. "Damn. I was gonna say 'good,' but I guess we both know better."

"What happened?" Smoke turned to his father's friend, his fingers clenched into a tight fist. "Why weren't they in the shelter? Dad dug it deep enough. Hell, it's big enough all five horses could've been down there with them. In a squeeze, the mules would've fit, too. They would've been safe."

Jared's eyes fell to his boots. "There's no way of knowing. The twister only touched down in a couple places. It never once settled to walk the prairie like some of 'em do. It wasn't a wedge, just a long skinny finger, but it was a mean SOB. Your dad might've been making sure his horses were safe for all I know. He might've thought he had more time. I'm sorry. Go get some rest."

Smoke nodded once. International flights were exhausting all by themselves, but the turmoil that came with being a sole survivor? Damned wearing on a man's soul. "Thanks."

There was nothing more to say. Jared headed to that dusty Chevy pickup Smoke had parked behind while he walked into his parent's home.

He walked straight to his old man's tool shed off the expansive red brick patio. The moment the door cracked open, it struck him. The smell of gasoline, the tidy order of tools and equipment, all of it waited for the wrong man. Ducking inside, the claustrophobic sensation tightened like a noose around his neck. He was back under his dad's thumb again, young and dumb, being educated in the one and only way to do things, the Caleb Montoya way, and shit. He didn't want to deal with his old man's my-way-or-the-highway mentality ever again.

Steeling his nerve, Smoke located the chainsaw. He grabbed a pair of safety glasses and gloves from the workbench and hurried back to the fallen giants along the driveway, one in particular. Some things couldn't wait.

Back at the tree, he braced a boot to what had once been a leafy branch. Leveling the lightweight saw, he sliced a foot-by-foot section into the dense trunk, then a sideways swath that went six-inches deep. He couldn't risk breaking this one.

The blade bit evenly. His hand was steady. The pleasant odor of fresh sawdust drifted into his nose, but at last, he pulled the churning, biting chain free and set the saw aside. Dusting his hands, he lifted the square chunk of wood from the trunk and blew the sawdust clear of the memento he'd carved long ago.

The letters were gray and weathered, dried, not as deep as they'd been when his pocketknife had first bit through the hardwood. But deep enough. They'd lasted. That was what mattered.

S. M. and J. W.

He dusted off the telling word in the middle of the carved heart with the tip of his little finger, a brave word for a sixteen-year-old boy to declare in secret to the twelve-year-old girl who'd never looked twice at him. But like his enlistment in the Navy, this word still felt right.

Loves.

Chapter Three

After a restless first night home in a house that felt strange and empty, Smoke woke to the raucous whine of chainsaws and heavy engines. He rolled off the couch where he'd fallen asleep with the TV on and padded barefoot to the front door to see what the hell. He'd no more than cracked it open when the scent of sawdust and morning filled his nose.

It wasn't just Smitty Ferguson out there. Looked like he'd brought a crew with him. They'd all shown up too damned bright and early, decked out in jeans and work boots, and were already manning limb saws and chainsaws. Safety glasses and helmets, too. But they also looked like they knew what they were doing.

Damned if one of the guys didn't shoot him a proper military salute from his perch atop the oak nearest the front porch. "We wake you, princess?" he bellowed over the noise of his chainsaw, a big shitty smile on his face. Black-haired and dark-eyed, he could've passed for Smoke's brother—except for that grin.

Smoke returned to the house, scrambled into his boots, not yet ready for a day of logging the debris field that his parent's property had been turned into. But ready or not, he had a full crew at his disposal. He intended to use them.

Back outside, Jared waved him over to where he stood with old man Ferguson. "You're going to need these," he yelled as he handed over a set of earphones and a pair of safety glasses.

Smitty grabbed onto Smoke's hand before he could don the gear. "I hope you don't mind, but when I heard you were home, I made a few calls. When they heard it was you who needed help, they couldn't get here fast enough."

Whatever that meant.

"I just want these trees chipped and cleared out," Smoke ordered over the noise of saws and men shouting orders to each other. "Don't go to any extra trouble on my account. This is all salvage lumber as far as I'm concerned."

Smitty half-nodded before he changed directions and shook his head in outright denial. His clear gray eyes drilled Smoke's. "Trust me to know my business, young man. This beautiful wood is not meant for chipping. Oak this clean is worth a small fortune. Look at the rings in that log alone, and it's one of the smaller ones."

Smoke looked to the monster log that had rolled free from the nearest downed tree. That six-foot-wide behemoth was a small one? He got the point, but he wanted this done and over with. He wasn't interested in making a profit, just getting out of town.

Smitty's brows furrowed. "To treat these giants like salvage lumber would be a waste and a crime. I cannot do it. No, no. At least let me give you something from this awful catastrophe. It's the least I can do. I'll pay you what they're worth. You'll see."

Both Smoke's palm came up. "No, sir. No way. I don't want profit." *I just want gone.*

Smitty winked. "Trust me. I'll take especially good care of you."

"Hey stranger," a particularly ramrod straight man interrupted the difference of opinion, his stride straight and true and headed Smoke's way. "Damn, you're a sight for sore eyes."

"Joseph?" Smoke couldn't believe his eyes. Joseph Klein. Mid-forties. Dark hair sprinkled with gray. He ran the local gym where Smoke had once decided boxing was not for him. "These your guys?"

"Some of 'em. Smitty's got his own boys working around here somewhere." Joseph brushed Smoke's handshake aside and went straight for the throat. With a jerk, Smoke was inside his old friend's embrace, his eyes full of something that stung, his back getting pounded good and hard. "Damn sorry this happened. Coming home had to be hard for you."

Smoke choked at the outright compassion in his friend's voice. "Yeah, well... Yeah."

Joseph let him go, keeping it real, and pointed to the guy atop the nearest oak. "When Smitty called, I pulled in everyone I know. I asked them if they were up to a tough job for a friend, and here we are. That smart ass up there's Scotty Ferguson. He's former military. You'll like him. He's another go-getter just like you. My boy Tex is around here somewhere, and—"

"Here!" a lean, dark-haired guy yelled from deep inside the same oak Scotty commandeered. "You want these cut in eight- or ten-foot lengths?"

Smitty hurried off to direct his crews, leaving Jared standing there with his hands on his hips and a satisfied smirk on his face. He winked, damn him. The old codger winked.

Smoke had to nod, accepting the truth behind that subtle 'I told you so' wink. People did care.

Joseph continued the intros, strolling with his palm planted firmly on Smoke's shoulder.

"You don't need to do this," Smoke protested. He needed a cup of coffee, maybe two before he could deal with all this—charity.

"Why not? This is what we do. We pitch in and we help out. Don't worry." Joseph pointed toward the two lumbering flatbeds parked on the road, their trailers ready to accept the lumber. "If we don't finish today, we'll be back tomorrow."

What's a tough guy supposed to say? Smoke rolled his shoulders and prepared to do his fair share of the hauling, cutting, and sweating. But damn. All this neighborly pitching-in was hard to accept.

"Feels good, don't it?" Jared growled at him when he came back for the safety gear.

Smoke had to admit. Smitty and Joseph's crews knew what they were doing. Clem and Betty, his only neighbors within miles, had yet to show up, so having these strangers on hand felt damned good. "Do you know a Jenkins Lassiter? He left a flyer stuck in one of the trees; said he wanted to buy the ranch. What the hell's happened to this town? We're building casinos now?"

Jared shook his head. "Not if the city council has anything to say about it. Don't trust Lassiter. He's got more commercials on TV about his uppity ideas for Sunnyvale than Carters has pills. Talk is he's fighting the planning commission to rezone your neighbor's property."

"Hardy's place? Why? They move?" *Already?* Smoke's head swiveled to the ranch west of The Chaparral.

"Word is they sold out the day after the twister hit. You know Clem. He'd squeeze a nickel if he thought it would shit a dime."

That explained why Clem and Betty weren't here. "Where'd they move to?"

Jared lifted one shoulder. "They didn't say, but I'm guessing Big Springs. That's where their daughter lives."

Smoke stuck his chin at the men in his yard. "Are these the same guys who helped Ethan?" He wanted to thank them if they were. Ethan had been his long-time buddy, one of the few who'd written during his time in SEAL Team 2. But guy-letters never told enough. There were so many things left unsaid. So many questions Smoke wished he'd asked while he'd had the chance.

Jared shook his head. "No, those guys were the local paramedics. They came out the day after the accident and removed the tree so Jessie wouldn't have to deal with it when she got home. They did a good job cleaning the yard up. She'll never know where it happened."

A knot climbed up Smoke's throat. "She's coming home?"

"I haven't heard for certain yet, but I hope so. No one knows how to get a hold of her. Do you?"

"Sure don't." *Wish I did, though.* Smoke stared at the quiet home to the east of the hacienda, his heart thumping faster, harder than usual. *Jess's coming home.* Through many long deployments he'd wished he'd had her number. Now he'd have to go over and extend his condolences. *Maybe extend something more...*

The guys broke for an early lunch at ten. By then, a group of women had arrived with lunch. In no time at all, they laid a mountain of sandwiches on a picnic table that sprang up from nowhere. They'd also filled a galvanized tub with ice, bottled water, and soda. Someone had thought ahead and brought enough chairs for the crew to rest while they ate. Jared made the rounds, filling empty coffee cups and coordinating the afternoon schedule between Smitty and Joseph. The ranch looked and felt like one big picnic of lumberjacks, muscle, and brawn. The camaraderie and friendly guy banter took Smoke back to his days in the Navy. His parent's house almost—almost—felt like home again.

By noon, more of Smitty's guys arrived with a pneumatic scissors-lift to move the logs. The log loader they'd brought earlier grabbed the ten-foot oak lengths and transferred them easily to the heavy-duty flatbeds lining the road. A John Deere log-skidder made the heavy job smooth, easy, and quick.

The sheriff stopped by with a 'hey' and more condolences. He didn't stay long enough for Smoke to chat, but left when he'd received a home invasion call. By midafternoon, Smoke had the makings of a driveway again. At least, the path was clear. The heavy equipment had left ruts aplenty in the saturated ground, but he knew how to work his old man's tractor. Ruts were nothing to fix.

By early afternoon, the last of the logs were on their way to Smitty and Sons and the mounds of sawdust had been raked into a manageable mulch pile at the side of the hacienda. The sandwiches were gone, and the kitchen had been left neat and clean. Joseph's and Smitty's crews had both packed up and left. Even Jared and the ladies were gone.

Smoke stood on his mother's porch with his hands on his hips. No trace remained of the noisy charity work except for a clear path for a new driveway and a box of twelve cupcakes on the table labeled: *Don't touch. These are for Smoke Only.* That and a raft of homemade sandwiches tucked into zippered bags in his fridge.

It was more than Smoke had ever expected and more than he could begin to repay. He didn't know most of these guys that showed up and worked their guts out. For sure, this had been no easy day. Every last one of those men had to be hammered after the physical labor they'd put in. Why'd people do that? Be kind to strangers? Be thoughtful? Be friends when a guy they didn't know least expected it? When he needed it most?

Smoke coughed at what felt like a hard fist stuck in his throat. The sun hovered low in the Texas sky. The shadows were long and his first day at home was done. Once again, the hacienda felt empty. Bleak.

He went back inside for one of those sandwiches.

Chapter Four

Jessie placed her palm to her brother's front room picture window, the next dilemma of this crappy week on the rampage all over the front lawn. Literally. On. The. Rampage.

Ethan's damned prized cattle were loose. Texas longhorns. His babies. The only thing keeping them off the road at the moment was the thin line of barbed wire running along the gravel shoulder. It wasn't even electrified. Biting back tears, she ran her fingers through her ebony tangles. Bone-tired and weary to her soul, she hadn't come to grips with the empty house or the monumental task of a funeral ahead of her, and now this. Too much!

God must really hate me.

It seemed everyone wanted a piece of her. The lady from the funeral parlor needed clothes to bury Ethan in. Jessie stalled, the final task of going through his closet too difficult for the tender state of her broke heart. But there was no choice. Ethan needed to be dressed, so she'd ended up in his room, pairing his dress slacks with both of his dress shirts, then his western shirts with his newest jeans. In the end, she couldn't bear seeing his things, touching his laundered clothes. Unable to decide which outfit better personified her brother's outlook on life, she'd before she suffocated with regret for all the things she couldn't change.

She'd was no more than downstairs, thinking to hide from the world in her bedroom, when some pushy real estate agent called, again. Mr. Lassiter. What a jerk. He'd called three times—three!—since she'd arrived home. What was he, a stalker watching the ranch through a long-distance lens? He wanted to discuss the sale of her brother's, ahem, *her* ranch. But why now? Why not wait until after the funeral? This was her first day home. Wasn't there some kind of time limit, where folks were allowed to grieve before they had to deal with life again?

To get him off the phone, she'd outright lied and told him she was her personal assistant, that he'd have to call back when Jessie West came to town. *Thank you, goodbye, and good riddance.*

But then he'd called back, asking if Jessie'd made it home yet. The nerve! It took a while to settle down after those disturbing calls. The man was too persistent and way too cheerful, as if something as trivial as Ethan's death, wouldn't stand in the way of his plans for some ungodly casino.

Oh, God, her heart ached. It actually hurt to breathe. If that wasn't enough, her stomach clenched with more acid at what her deception would mean to this town if word got out that she'd already come home. What a story that would make: *Local Girl Makes It Big, Then Snubs Hometown.* Jessie needed an antacid. Make that a double. Maybe a bottle.

Turning away from the window, her heart shattered all over again. She'd didn't want to deal with the press. They had a way of launching preemptive strikes and assassinating their victims before they knew the facts. Not that truth mattered to the media. Hardly. She'd learned that lesson early.

When this story got out, they'd run her down and trump-up more sensational lies to sell their stories. Once again, she'd be nobody. Worse, she'd be nobody with a ruined reputation. Everyone would know what a spoiled, selfish diva she'd become. Too good for Sunnyvale. Maybe she had been the worst sister to the best brother in the world, and she'd have to live with that. But right now, she'd had enough. And she still had Ethan's cattle to deal with.

A bitter tear slid out of the corner of her eye. This first day home had taken more than she had to give but give she would. Those rangy cattle were punching post-hole-deep divots in her waterlogged lawn, and they wouldn't stop there. She could see the headlines now: *Super Model Jessie West and Her Free Roaming Longhorns. Lawsuits Filed. Punitive Damages in the Millions! New York's Problem Child in Trouble Again.*

It was enough to make a grown woman sit down and bawl—if she'd had the time. Jessie didn't. There was no choice. It was time to giddy-up and wrangle those doggies home.

Oh, wait. Maybe the Montoyas were home. Ethan's friend Smoke, didn't live there anymore, but surely a ranch hand would be hanging around.

Maybe Mr. Montoya. Caleb. He still owned horses, didn't he? He'd know what to do. How could he turn down a damsel in distress? This wasn't New York. People in Texas still helped each other, didn't they?

She honestly didn't know. It had been awhile since she'd been among simple country folks, but she meant to find out. Girding her loins, she pinned her hair up and donned the red-haired wig she'd brought with her, the same color as Barbara's. She topped that get-up with her floppy straw hat and a pair of oversized dark glasses. No one in Sunnyvale needed to know she was home, and she intended to keep it that way. Jessie transformed from a glamorous super-model to New Yorker and Girl Friday, Barbara Esposito.

Her capris made her look ordinary. So, did the simple button-up blouse she'd pulled out of the closet in her old bedroom. Why Ethan hadn't cleaned her things out of that room, repainted it, and turned it into a guy's mancave, amazed her. But his failure to move on also worked to her advantage. She hadn't brought many clothes with her, certainly nothing sturdy enough to herd cows. So she made do with the outfits she'd left behind. Then just to give the red-necked ensemble an ultra-feminine, poor-me spin, she added the six-inch heels she'd brought with her. She needed help, damn it, and all she had left was her feminine wiles, so this outfit had better work.

Jessie sized up her disguise in the first-floor bathroom mirror. Bad move. Ethan's things were everywhere. His electric shaver. His toothbrush. A curled tube of toothpaste with its cap off. His cologne, *Obsession*. But the ratty t-shirt tossed on the floor next to the hamper in typical Ethan-style was the last straw. Picking it up, she drew it to her nose and inhaled the scent she'd never know again, her heart breaking.

"I can't do this," she told her teary reflection in the mirror. "I don't want to bury my brother. Not by myself. It's too—" A sob hiccupped out of her. "It's too hard."

Wasn't that the truth? With that one phone call, her life had been turned upside down and inside out. Nothing made sense, not her crazy job back east or the way Ethan died. Not the longhorns grazing on her lawn, Mr. Lassiter, or the wretched pain tearing at her heart.

"Moo-o-o-o," some four-legged behemoth bellowed.

Damn it. She didn't have the luxury of feeling sorry for herself, and, news flash. There was nothing except Ethan's truck to get her to Montoyas, but it was a nightmare to climb up into, and a stick, something she had yet to master. That meant a long walk. In these stupid heels.

Rubbing her fingertips over her breastbone, she told Ethan, "Herding cattle would be fun if you were here. Why'd you have to go and get yourself killed by a tree?"

The cattle's hearty lowing tugged her out of the house and onto her front porch. Damn. Every last longhorn was heading west. Into the sunset. There was no choice now but to race them to Montoyas.

The breeze shifting up the walk brought fresh night air into her face. Jessie drew in the fragrance of the rich, fertile prairie, the sweet fragrance of the crepe myrtle growing beside the porch, and the earthy odors left behind by the wayward cattle.

Her broken heart cried out to her. *Home. I'm finally home, but I came too late. There's no reason to stay. There's nobody here to stay for.*

The truth sucked. Jessie beelined down her front walk and turned west at the gravel road. Why couldn't it be paved asphalt? Was the county road department that cheap? Probably because this was

Texas, where neighbors lived miles apart and traffic was sparse. Until What's-His-Name built that fancy casino. The county would probably build a four-lane highway then.

Discouraged, Jessie wanted to turn back time and make different choices. She wanted Ethan's monkey-bumps grinding on her head and a lip-smacking kiss on her cheek while she walked, not this empty feeling that she had nothing to live for. She wanted Smoke to tug at her pigtails again, to wink at her from under that dark shock of black hair like he had when they'd rodeoed together. She wanted her life back. Her real life, not the plastic, fake life she'd built for herself in NY, NY.

But life didn't work that way. For years, she and Ethan lived by themselves after their parents were both killed in a rollover on Interstate 30. She was fourteen when it happened. Ethan, eighteen. For a short while after that double funeral, her mother's father, Grandpa Evans came to live with them. But the uneasy truce between grandfather and grandson didn't last long. Grandpa moved out, probably because he was too old to deal with a rebellious upstart who thought he knew better, and who didn't appreciate his interference. But that was then. Grandpa Evans died from cancer a year later.

Now she had nothing left of Ethan's but this herd of rangy longhorns. Even they were ambling away from her. To greener grasses. To happier days. The story of her life.

By then the sun had dipped below the horizon, but Jessie kept walking, carefully avoiding the loose gravel that might make her trip, or worse, sprain an ankle. She wouldn't be surprised. It had been that kind of day.

Wouldn't you know? Headlights approached from the west, blinding her. She waved the driver down, relying on her helpless damsel in distress routine. Thank goodness, the cab slowed to a crawl, then a stop. Now for the real test. She needed to fool the cabbie.

He ended up being old man Stauffer, a well-known sight around Sunnyvale. His Ford van taxi always needed a tune-up. Half-tempted to tell him she could take care of that simple maintenance for him, when she wasn't busy pretending to be her personal assistant, Jessie bit her lip as his gaze locked onto her.

"Do you need a ride, young lady?" he asked while he eased his lanky frame onto the road. His hand reached out for hers, reminding her yet again that Texas was a world away from the NY.

Sparkling dark brown eyes gleamed from his equally dark skin. She'd always liked Mr. Stauffer. His chosen vocation seemed a perfect fit for a man who seemed to like everyone.

"Thank you, I do," she replied, adding a bit of Bronx to her voice as she shook his hand. "I'm going to the next ranch if you have time. The Montoyas. Do you know them?"

"I know everyone around these parts." His hand shifted to her elbow as he opened the passenger door for her. "I hope you don't mind riding up front with me, ma'am. I've got groceries in the back and a big box of blankets for the rescue mission."

The tension eased out of her. Mr. Stauffer might not recognize her, but he was familiar and just what she needed.

"No, not at all." She drew her long legs into the cab while he secured the door without slamming it. See? Chivalry wasn't dead. All those little things made the difference between being treated like a lady or just another fare. She dashed an errant tear out of the corner of her eye.

Mr. Stauffer was the only bright spot in a dismal day. He didn't pry, and she didn't offer much conversation during the short ride. As much as Jessie wouldn't have minded telling him who she was, she couldn't. For now, everyone needed to believe she was no one important, just the personal assistant to a high fashion diva, Barbara Esposito.

On the day of the funeral, Barbara Esposito would disappear and Jessie West would suddenly arrive in Sunnyvale. The word would be out by then, and no doubt, every fashion rag from the Atlantic to the Pacific, would have a reporter and a photographer in the house. There'd be mayhem. There'd be false condolences and feigned sympathy from fake friends who just wanted to be seen with her. There'd be those ever so disgusting photos of her breaking down and ruining her make-up when she told Ethan goodbye.

Jessie steeled her spine. The truth was, she didn't plan to stay longer than it took to bury her brother. After she was gone, her attorney would sell the West ranch, auction off those pesky cattle, and she'd leave Texas in the dust once more. This state always ended in heartache. She'd had enough to last a lifetime.

"There you are, young lady," Mr. Stauffer said congenially as he pulled into the Montoya's drive. The man had to be in his sixties. She offered a twenty for the cab-fare, but he brushed the bill aside. "Oh, pshaw. 'Tweren't nothing but a drive on a lovely spring evening with a pretty woman. I hardly used any gas. You save that for a rainy day. Should I wait for you?"

She ran her tongue over her bottom lip, counting on the Montoya's hospitality for that ride home. It was then she looked out her window. Her throat went dry. "Where are the trees? The driveway? Everything's gone."

Mr. Stauffer scraped a hand over his short gray hair. "Not everything. Look a little closer. The lights are off, but the rest of the ranch is still standing. Dangedest thing I've ever seen. That funnel hopped, skipped, and jumped over the rest of the county like it couldn't decide where to land. Then it stopped here and took just what it wanted. It's a wonder Caleb's sign's still standing, ain't it?"

"A tornado?" That explained Ethan's tree. It would've been nice if someone had told her that before now. She'd been so wrapped up in the drama of missing the shot in Cannes, all she'd heard was that Ethan had been killed in an accident. The shock of that had blocked other details.

"Yes, ma'am. A whopper of a tornado. Right here in little old Sunnyvale."

Jessie stared at the once elegant greeting to the lovely Montoya hacienda. Texans were known for their pride in state and country. They lived hard, they played harder, and everything they did, they did with pride and brash bravado. There wasn't a ranch in the county, maybe the whole state, that didn't boast some kind of gate at the edge of the property, preferably with a twelve-foot—at least— sign over the top that proclaimed family name, fealty to country, or some such swagger.

The solid oak Montoya welcome that Caleb installed years ago had been just as bold, the state's motto carved between two five-pointed Texas stars: *Teyshas!*—the Caddo Indian word for friends.

"How weird," she breathed. "The house is still here. The sign. The stables, but—" All the trees were gone. Just poof. Gone.

"Moo-o-o-o-o-o-o..."

Damn it. Ethan's pesky longhorns showed up, still trampling westward, still looking for greener pastures. Suddenly her disguise felt more like a cheap costume. A cruel joke. Jessie balked. If Mr. or Mrs. Montoya even hinted at Ethan's death, she'd fall apart, and where would she be then? Recognized and in trouble, that's where.

A solitary light flickered from the Montoya's front window. It had to be the television, but all those trees. It was as if they'd just disappeared.

Maybe this wasn't a good idea to come asking for help in the middle of the night from folks who'd already lost so much. Were Caleb and Caroline even okay? Did they know what happened to Ethan? Of course they did. Word travelled fast in Sunnyvale. They'd welcome her as if she were family and—

I don't know if I can do this.

Unfortunately, Mr. Stauffer hurried to open her door. "I can wait for you, young lady," he said, his hand extended to help her to her feet. "'Tain't no skin off my nose. You tend to your business, and I'll be here when you're ready to leave."

Like it or not., it was showtime. Accepting his hand, Jessie slid off the passenger seat to her feet. "No, I might be a while. I'll be okay," she said, not feeling it, but her sunglasses were still intact and her identity was safe. She hoped. Mr. Stauffer had been around forever, and she was surprised he hadn't recognized her. It would've been nice if he had. She could use a friend.

"Well, if you're sure." He gave her one last chance before he climbed back into the front seat and shut the cab door.

Jessie stiffened her spine and prepared to follow through. "Thanks anyway. You get those groceries home."

"Okay then." He left her there in the dark.

As the cab's red taillights flickered away, she climbed the three steps to the Montoyas front door, rang their doorbell, and waited for Caleb to answer, her throat tight and dry. This was the stupidest thing she'd ever done.

By then Ethan's herd was at home on the range, trampling what was left of the already rutted Montoya front lawn like they owned the place. Tapping her foot, she pressed the doorbell again. Maybe the bell was broken. She could still detect the dim, flashing light, though. They hadn't just left their TV on and gone out for the evening, had they?

Opening the screen with its elegant wrought iron handle, she banged on the heavy wooden door, immediately cringing at the noise. Like it or not, she needed help before those pesky steers took a walk on the wild side and caused real trouble.

Finally. A muffled noise sounded from the other side of the door.

Oh, good, someone was home. She swallowed hard, her dark glasses still intact. Still Barbara.

Wow. Fooling Mr. and Mrs. Montoya would be the biggest test of all.

Glancing at the bad boys milling around the yard, she panicked. There was still time to change her mind and run back home until—

The door opened inward. Someone growled. A massive shadow blocked the dim light from within. Wide shoulders. Rounded biceps. Deceptively languid strength coiled beneath a sleeveless tee. Okay, so he was rubbing sleep out of his eyes, but this wasn't Mr. Montoya. This was no ranch hand, either. No aw-shucks neighbor from the sticks whom she could fool.

Ah-uh. This was—him. The cowboy she'd worshipped when she'd been nothing but a skinny, awkward ten-year-old in braces and braids. Her one and only unrequited love. Her greatest crush. Her biggest mistake. Now the most beautiful male she'd ever seen. Smoke Montoya was home.

What's he doing here?

Jessie went perfectly still as warning bells in her head shrieked at her to hightail it off that porch and run! But even as she contemplated doing that, her throbbing heart dropped with a hearty splat to the brick porch as the clean scent of male deodorant and body wash drifted out the door. She could barely breathe much less speak. Smoke was too near. Too handsome. Too—everything.

His hair glistened in the dark, the sides trimmed short, but the top longer, spilling into his eyes. Still black as raven wings. Still straight as his Spanish heritage. *Probably still soft, too.*

The most delicious impulse rippled up her thighs to her belly and right up her throat, clamping it shut. Like a deer paralyzed in an eighteen wheeler's headlights, Jessie's initial inclination to hide fought with her overwhelming need to climb into Smoke's surprised arms and kiss the hell out of him.

He grumbled in an aggravated bass so deep that it plucked shivers up the back of her neck, "Yeah? What can I do for you?"

Maybe not.

Her carefully laid plan to deceive the Montoyas crumbled to ash. This was her brother's best bud, and the boy who'd once known her better than any of her girlfriends. The one she'd given her heart to, but never told.

One delicious bare arm curled over his head, spiking his hair with a backward sweep over his skull. Veins stood out on his thickly-corded bare bicep, daring her to touch. "Excuse me, ma'am, but I asked if you needed something."

"Umm…" The sight of all that raw masculinity fried every last circuit on her pathetic logic card. "Umm…"

Still blinking, he grunted, the most musical sound she'd heard in ages. "Listen lady. It's late and I've had a long day." He toed the door open wider and flipped on the yellow porch light, peering into her face. "Who are you anyway? Whatcha selling this time of night?"

A teleprompter would've come in handy. "I'm, umm…" But coherent speech failed to materialize.

No man looked more achingly beautiful than the disgruntled male standing there on Caroline Montoya's porch in workout pants with sleep in his eyes. Instinctively, her fingers itched to caress the scruffy edge of his jaw. To tunnel into the softness of his hair. To soothe a fraction of the blatant anguish etched at the corners of his tired eyes. Laugh lines used to linger there. Where had they gone?

She kept her hands to herself. "I was told Caleb Montoya lived here."

Darkness drifted over Smoke's rugged face. A veneer of ice. Of graveyards and ghouls. "He's dead," he said, a point-blank shot to her heart.

"Wh-what happened?" she stuttered, sorry that she'd come.

Poor Smoke stood there as alone as she was, as angry as ever, a lost soul. Like her. Her heart reached out to him, needing to invite him in, though she was the one on his step. Needing to grab hold of him and hang on for dear life.

Jessie stopped herself just in time, opting to pat her ridiculous curly wig instead. She'd better get a grip or this idiotic idea would be for nothing.

Swallowing hard, she just needed this nightmare day to end. For two cents, she'd leave the drama of her high-powered life behind. Instead of a diva, she'd be simple, fun-loving Jessie West again. She'd pull Smoke into her arms and cry with him. But she couldn't.

There was nothing left of the boy she'd once taunted on the rodeo circuit. This guy was all male, built of hard stone and dark shadows, decisions both made by him and for him. Bathed in the golden glow of the porch light, he hadn't offered a hint of a smile, much less recognition.

"Moo-o-o," some idiot steer bellowed.

CHAPTER FIVE

S moke peered into the darkness beyond this strange lady's fuzzy head. She looked like a clown standing there on his mom's porch in sunglasses, strappy high-heeled sandals at the stroke of what had to be midnight. Her collarbones stuck out like she hadn't eaten in a while. Her cheeks were gaunt, her arms too skinny. She could've passed for a scarecrow in that get-up.

He'd fallen asleep to the backdrop of the national news, but now wide-awake, he brushed past the stuttering gal on his porch, needing to understand what the hell had just moved out there in the dark. *Shit. Are those longhorns in my yard?* Sure as hell, somebody had left their pasture gate open, and he had another mess to clean up.

Smoke stabbed an angry finger at the restless trespassers. "Are those yours?" he asked the woman.

"God, no. They're my bro... umm, my client's brother's, and I d-d-don't know how they got out, b-b-but—" A hollow chuckle peeled off her lips.

"Cows, nothing. Those are Texas longhorns, ma'am," he bit out, recognizing the nearly seven-foot span of horns on the nearest steer, a black and white brindle eyeing his mother's geraniums. "Scram!" he yelled, waving the beast away. *Holy shit! Look at the mess they're making.*

"I, umm, need help rounding them up and heading them out." She added an affected city-girl twang to her plight.

"And how do you propose *we* do that?" he shot at her, testing the twang that had unexpectedly resonated deep in his gut. Make that his groin. There was something familiar to this foolish woman, something he couldn't put his finger on. The red hair bugged him. "You ride?"

Stabbing her index fingers to the bridge of those ridiculous sunglasses, she replied, "Why no-o-o-o, I never—"

"Fine. Stay here then. Whatever you do, don't let them get to the road before I get back." Slapping a palm to his thigh, he growled at the day that just... Would. Not. End.

Smoke was caught in a nightmare, and that ninny of a woman would be no damned help. He'd have to wrangle those longhorns by himself, and it was late, and he was beat, and... *Damn!*

Back in the house, he shoved out of the workout pants he'd put on after his shower and pushed back into his dirty jeans and work boots. On impulse, he snagged his father's cowboy hat off the hook by the door and slapped it on his head. The damned thing fit, and just that fast, Smoke was a kid again, wanting to be just like Dad. Memories sucked. Big time.

Back at the porch, a wave of déjà vu tumbled over him. His blood stirred at the sight of that feminine profile. Miss Barbara was that missing word on the tip of his tongue, that elusive answer to the million-dollar question. Oddly familiar. Strangely indecipherable. Elusive.

He had to ask, "Do I know you?"

Her chin tilted up as she flashed a mouthful of perfect pearly whites. "A gal can only wish, big fella."

Again with that annoying chuckle. It grated his last nerve. *Give me a break. A come-on? Really?* In the middle of what, with one flash of lightning, could easily turn that meandering herd into a rip, roaring stampede? He didn't have time for her brand of bullshit, not as fast as those steers were peppering, make that splattering, his yard with it.

"Come with me," he ordered, setting a brisk pace to the stable. It'd sure be nice if Jared had returned, but Smoke doubted he'd be that lucky. Opening the stable door slowly, he extended his arm, feeling for the string dangling from the single bulb mounted at the ceiling fixture. "Easy," he murmured, keeping his tone steady to not frighten the horses. "It's just me."

"Ooooooooo, it's dark in here," Jess's assistant fussed, her fingernails digging into his bicep.

No shit. "Yeah, well it's nighttime." What'd she expect?

With all the money his old man made, you'd think Caleb would've installed decent lights in the stable, but no. Smoke's dad's life was a study in doing things the cheapest, hardest way possible. Smoke cussed until he caught hold of the string and gave it a yank, careful not to elbow the annoying gal hovering too close for comfort at his side, the nervy one with her fingertips now square on his hip, the only ticklish spot on his body. He stepped away to break the intimate contact she had no business making. *Stupid woman.*

With the light on, instant calm filled the stable. The outside door was always left open, so the horses could come and go as they pleased. But all were inside the inner pen, shifting nervously at the late night interruption, their heads lowered.

All except Chip. The Appaloosa reared back, his nostrils flared. Mesquite, the bay with four white stockings, ambled out of the stable. She was smart like that, and not the friendliest of the five. Gentle Tango, the honey-gold palomino, nickered at the rail, while Brandy and Montana, the paints, perked their ears forward.

Mental note to self: *Bring carrots next time. These kids deserve a treat.*

Jared's care of the Montoya horses showed. Their coats gleamed in the soft sixty-watt glow, and their swishing tails were long and full. Chip's swept the ground. If nothing else, Caleb Montoya had been a damned good judge of horseflesh and hired hands.

"Sorry boy," Smoke groused as he took hold of Chip's and pretty girl Tango's halters. "I know it's late, but we've got work to do."

It didn't take long to saddle the horses. Smoke shut the stable doors and handed the mare's reins to the woman. "Here, take these. What'd you say your name was?"

She shook her head, her palms up to refuse the offer. "Barbara Esposito. You can call me Barbie. I'm Jessie West's assistant. I'm here for the funeral, but uh-uh, I don't ride."

"You're kidding? Jess couldn't make her own brother's funeral?" *Un-frickin'-believable.*

"No, that's not what I meant. Jessie's coming. She's just not here, umm, yet."

Whatever. Smoke stiffened his arm, the reins extended, his order clear. Jess West and her highfaluting ways were not at the top of his I-give-a-shit list, but Ms. Esposito was. She *would* learn to ride, and she'd learn it fast. Right damned now.

"Listen, Barbie," he all but growled. "We've got a herd of steers on the loose, and I can't do this alone. Just take hold of the reins and get up on Tango. I'll help you. All you have to do is what I tell you."

She balked, but he cut her no slack. He didn't have time for New York City, not tonight. Once those longhorns hit the road, the stakes upped exponentially. The law of the range ruled in Texas, but Smoke couldn't chance someone driving along in the dark and broadsiding one of those big animals. God, what if a family came by with a carload of kids tonight? Even a slow rate of speed would put one of those animals through the windshield. People could die.

He took a step toward Jess's assistant, pissed at her as much as her uppity, too-good-for-Texas boss. "We've got to get those cattle back in their pasture before someone gets killed."

"Well-l-l-l-l-l-l..." She stretched out that word like she was acting cute, but she accepted the reins. "Okay." At least she hadn't chuckled. That laugh of hers had gotten old.

"Left..." He started to tell her which side to mount the mare from, but for a greenhorn, Barbara guessed right. She'd already latched onto the saddle horn, slid her high-heeled foot into the stirrup like she knew what she was doing. But then she froze. She jerked away from Tango, stepped down and backed up like she'd been stung. Her nose twitched, bumping those ridiculous glasses up higher on her nose. "Exactly what do I, umm, do?"

Shit. He didn't have time for this. Dropping Chip's reins, he strode to her side. Tucking his hands to her slender waist, he was tired, pissed, and fed up with her turn-about-face and...

Shit. There it was again. The sensation that he'd done this exact same thing before. Somewhere.

Smoke leaned away to take another look at the feminine body caught in his work-roughened hands, sure he'd held this thin-as-a-rail woman in another lifetime. That he knew these boyish hips. The warmth from her body zipped up his arms like a line of hungry flames following a stream of gasoline. His throat went dry. He'd never had jetlag this bad before.

Needing to get those pesky cattle behind the wire before all hell broke loose, he shook it off. It would only take one car to turn this night into a disaster. The clock was ticking.

Hoisting Barbie What's-Her-Name's ass into the saddle made matters worse. Scents of leather and straw met his nostrils, but something else, too. Chocolate and orange peels, a vaguely familiar fragrance. His exhausted brain time-warped back to barrel racing, bronco busting and little kids dressed in chaps chasing after goats and...

That girl. The one who'd kept a secret stash of chocolate-covered orange sticks in an old ammo box under her bed. The one who grew up and moved away to be a big-city star.

He took a second hard look at Miss Barbie while she fussed with the reins she seemed to know precisely how to hold. Reins that looked natural and loose in her pretty manicured fingers. Not tight like a greenhorn would've held them.

"Do I know you?" he asked, needing to get his head out of the clouds.

She bounced in the saddle instead of looking at him, kicking Tango's sides, urging the mare forward. "Don't think so."

"Hold on a sec," he grumbled, grasping Tango's halter before this idiot woman took off into the dark and riled the strays. Man, she was dense. "Rule one. Don't kick this horse. Her name's Tango, and she's as gentle as a lamb. Tug the reins to the right to get her turned around, while I mount up, but take it easy. She's got a soft mouth. Stay behind me and follow my lead. Together, we'll brush Ethan's herd back the way they came. You're sure they're his?"

Miss Barbie's fuzzy head bobbed. "They're prize longhorns. Worth hundreds of thousands. He's been breeding them a couple years now."

That voice. Smoke narrowed his gaze, needing to see beyond the bizarre get-up. For a personal assistant from New York City, Miss Espinoza sure knew a lot about Ethan's business. *Hmmm.*

Mounting Chip, Smoke directed the horse the long way around the herd, keeping the ditsy woman between the road and the cattle. "I'll push them back the way they came. If they try to get past you, tap Tango's sides with the stirrups and block their path. Gently. She'll take it from there. Can you do that?"

Damned if she didn't cut Tango to the right and take up her post like she knew precisely where to go and what to do.

Clicking his tongue, Smoke eased Chip toward the black and white brindle, the steer that had gotten farthest west. "Come on. Hey now," he soothed, his voice low, urging the bad boy east. "Walk's over. You're going home."

The brindle lowered his impressive rack and snorted, not challenging, more annoyed he hadn't made it into the Montoya garden yet. When he turned his caboose around, the rest of the herd followed. Out of the corner of his eye, Smoke caught Barbara calmly and slowly waving her straw hat as she paralleled the herd to keep them off the road. *Greenhorn, my ass.*

The West's front porch light glimmered across the way.

"Don't rush them," he said softly, thankful there were no clouds in the sky and no chance of thunder or lightning to spook the herd. Traditionally, Caleb Montoya had left the field between the West and Montoya ranch, fallow, making this journey home easier.

Smoke settled into the gentle sway of Chip's easy gait and the peace of an unexpected late night ride. This was what he'd missed. The prairie. His home state. All those stars overhead. The fireflies flashing along the road side. Taking a deep breath, he willed his troubles away. "How many years?"

"Excuse me?" Miss What's-Her-Name asked, leaning over Tango's saddle horn like an experienced cowhand, instead of some novice from the East Coast. "How many years what?"

"How many years did you say Ethan owned this herd?" Smoke let his Texas drawl out for the first time in a while, enjoying the easy creak of leather and the steady hoof fall of good quarter horses. The night was clear and he was a cowboy again. Life didn't get better than this, and it hit him hard. He'd missed his home state. Maybe even his folks.

"Two, umm, years," Barbara said with a definite hitch in her voice, almost as if she were grieving for Jess's brother. "The white one up ahead of you was his first. Then he had to have another. Kind of like potato chips, he couldn't have just one. These are all steers and cows. The bull's in another... umm... I mean..." She sputtered and coughed, fluttering her fingers to her mouth as if she'd just said a whole lot more than she'd intended. "At least that's what Jessie told me, umm, I mean, Miss West."

Smoke kept on keeping on, but he did twist around in his saddle and shoot one deadly round of truth at Miss High-And-Mighty herself. "Good to see you again, Jess. You little liar."

Chapter Six

Damn. *He knows.* Nudging Tango in the sides, Jessie closed the distance between her and that smug cowboy sitting tall in the saddle ahead of her. "Let me guess," she groused as she stuck the stem of her Hollywood sunglasses in her shirt, then dragged the hat and wig off, loosening the tangled mass of ebony curls she'd trapped beneath the red. "You knew it was me all along."

Smoke grunted, the clump of horse hooves peaceful on this moonless night. "You can't hide who you are, Jess."

"But I don't want anyone to know I'm in town. You can't tell. Promise."

He cocked a spiked brow, sharp enough she could see it beneath the brim of his cowboy hat. Smoke looked good in that old Stetson, just as stern as his father, Caleb. The resemblance was breathtaking. "You'd rather folks think you're too shallow to attend your only brother's funeral?"

She blew out a testy sigh. "I don't care what folks around here think."

"Sure you do. That's why you're here. You care what Ethan would think, too."

"You don't want to be here, either," she guessed. "You'd rather not be home."

"You're right, but my reasons are different than yours. My dad and I disagreed on fundamental values. On heart. When he told me never to come home again, he meant it. I just gave him what he asked for."

"And my parents died," she said defensively, "and all I had left was Ethan. If the press finds out I'm here, they'll be all over me, and I'm so sick of—"

"Being something you're not?" Smoke snorted, his words hanging between them like bright golden nuggets of truth.

"Something like that," she murmured. "They'll turn his funeral into a media zoo. Trust me. It'll make the front page of every fashion rag in the world and the press will spoil everything."

"Are you really *that* popular?" It was hard to miss the sarcasm dripping off his lips.

"You have no idea." Notorious was a better word. Driven. What had started out as an impossible dream come true had turned into something else. She hated herself and her job, most of the people in the modeling industry, too. It really was a dog-eat-dog world, one she didn't belong in anymore.

"Why don't you tell 'em to go to hell if you're so miserable?"

She closed her eyes, her grip comfortable on Tango's saddle horn. Ten years earlier this ride home would've been the perfect end to a teenage girl's day, but that girl had learned life's lessons the hard way. "It's not that easy. Believe it or not, I've worked hard to get where I am in this business. People depend on me. My agent. My publicist. My makeup artists. They'd all be out of work if I up and quit. It'd be a scandal of mega proportions. I've got contracts and commitments and—"

"You won't quit because you like it," he said gruffly, his back to her and the longhorns still headed to their field. He made this task of capturing wayward cattle look effortless. And sad…

"Of course I do, but it's not that easy." Didn't this guy get it?

He pulled his horse up short, the reins tight enough that Chip cut back and nickered in surprise. Smoke turned in his saddle, one hand on the cantle, the rear of the saddle seat. "You don't fool me, so stop lying to yourself. You like modeling. You like being a big star, and you like the press and all the attention. You always have. That's why the talent contests and beauty shows when you were just a kid. That's why the Miss Texas and Miss America pageants. If you didn't like the modeling circuit, you wouldn't do it, so stop bitching. Man up and call it what it is. You won't quit because then you wouldn't be some rich bitch living high on the East Coast. You wouldn't be important, would you? You'd be ordinary—like the rest of us."

"Wow. Tell me how you really feel, why don't you?" she sniped back at him, her feelings hurt even as she recognized the ring of truth to his words. There was a time she'd craved the world's praise, but back then, she'd been searching for her place in the whole scheme of things. Not now.

He kicked Chip into a gallop, his parting shot on the wind. "A gal who's too chicken shit to honor her dead brother sure as hell didn't deserve him."

She swallowed hard. That went well. Not.

Jessie plodded back to her empty house on Tango, needing to explain to the bossy guy she used to have feelings for, but who now thought he knew everything, when in fact, Smoke knew nothing about her. Not anymore. But by the time she caught up with him, he had the longhorns back in their field, all except one mischievous red. The big guy sidestepped the gate at the last moment and bobbed back and forth like he couldn't decide which way to run.

She settled her arm over Tango's saddle horn and leaned in to watch the impromptu contest between the man who was known as one of America's most lethal snipers and that single head of lean beef that decided he wanted to play tag.

Red chucked to the right, but Smoke's quick-footed cow horse cut the steer off. Smoke clung to his ride easily like the expert bronc buster he'd once been, riding low, his fingers easy on the reins and his sharp black eyes on the prize. It did Jessie's heart good to see him back in the saddle again. She could almost believe nothing had changed.

After a grunt and another feint, this time to Red's left, Smoke slapped his thigh, shouted, and the plucky steer gave up the contest. Red ducked through the gate, his horns lowered and snorting his druthers with a long string of spit drooling off his snout—but in he went.

Smoke slid to the ground while Chip, still one of the best cow ponies ever, stayed put at the exit. Swinging the pasture gate closed, Smoke looped the chain twice through the catch before any other longhorns changed their minds. With Chip at his back, he doffed his cowboy hat and ran a hand over his head.

If ever there was a picture-perfect moment, this was it. The ambient light of the starry night gleamed off his shiny black hair like molten silver off raven wings. He stared the grumbling herd on the other side of the fence down, a silhouette of man against beast, a stunning profile of cowboy against the cattle drive.

The same fire as before commenced glowing deep in Jessie's gut.

Smoke's shoulders were broader, thicker than she remembered. His back seemed straighter, his waist as lean and as narrow as ever. His legs were long and trim, his thighs thick. This was no longer the boy she and Ethan used to run with. This was one hundred percent man, from the jut of his stubborn chin the dust on his plain black work boots. He held his chin high and his back ramrod straight against the world. Smoke Montoya had changed into one splendid specimen of the male gender. But not a hint of her friend remained.

Her breath stalled in her throat, stuck so high she couldn't swallow. No wonder he'd joined the Navy. He always did know what he stood for. *Truth. Justice. The American way.* Yes, he reminded her of Superman.

When Tango whinnied, Jessie's fingers instinctively gripped the reins. She wanted to tug Smoke's hair the way she used to, just to get his attention off the longhorns and back on her. It was too bad the disagreement over her modeling career came up like it had. She didn't want to argue. Not tonight. Not when they'd both lost so much.

"You look good, cowboy," she offered honestly, hoping things could go back the way they were. That she and Smoke could be innocent kids again with a brighter, at least a friendlier, future ahead of them. That they could go back in time and make different choices. He could come home from the wars a welcomed hero instead of a castoff son.

She'd give up her foolish dream of being Miss Popular. The life of a supermodel wasn't all it was cracked up to be. She knew that now. Surely there was a better, a wiser way forward for both of them. Maybe they could work this mess out together?

Smoke didn't respond, just grabbed Chip's reins with an impatient jerk.

"Do you ever think about us?" she asked quietly, her voice as small and sad as this unfortunate homecoming made her feel.

He shook his head, his eyes on the saddle as he swung a leg over Chip's broad back and held out his hand for her to give up Tango's reins. He couldn't have hurt her worse when he growled, "If you don't mind, I'm tired. It's been a long day. I'm going home."

As in alone.

"Now who's lying?" she bit out. "You're not tired. You're running away."

CHAPTER SEVEN

Jess never knew when to shut up. That stubborn streak of hers might have gotten her far in the high fashion modeling circuit, but not here in Texas, and especially not after a day like this one. The nerve of her to skulk into town in disguise. To pretend to be her personal assistant. How stupid did she think he was? Miss *Stuck-Up Jessie West* had another thing coming, and Smoke meant to give it to her.

She still hadn't relinquished Tango's reins, but he no longer cared. In two quick easy seconds, he dropped off Chip's saddle on his way to set things straight. Ethan deserved better than a snot-nosed little sister who thought more of herself than she did him.

With a snort, Smoke dragged her ass off Tango, his hands clenched tight on her biceps while he decided if he should kill her or shake sense into her. Kiss her or spank the shit out of her. Inadvertently, his fingertips sifted through the cool, silky tangles and ebony shadows of... All. That. Hair.

His nostrils flared wide, drawing in the flowery, feminine essence of her hairspray and the spring breeze, temptation and satisfaction meshed together in a heady reminder of days past.

"I loved my brother," she declared hoarsely, her chin up and sad defiance glittering in her eyes. "And I didn't come back here because I'm the selfish bitch you and the rest of the world think I am. I came here to honor Ethan in *my* way, Smoke. *My way!* Privately. Quietly. Without all of New York City looking over my shoulder through a wide-angled lens, and without a dozen cameras in my face to catch every tear. Without his death being turned into a cheap publicity stunt to make me look good, so they can sell more products. You don't know what it's like!"

Damn. Not a quiver in her. Not a hint of fear. Not even a hint that she was smart enough to back off and stop leading with that chin of hers. Or that sweet drift of chocolate covered orange on her breath. Citrus and decadence. He could look at her forever and never get enough.

Starlight blinked in her eyes, a universe he never meant to explore until...

"You're too damned skinny," he bit out, needing to catch himself before he fell. He'd never stood a chance against her tough little girl persona, and damned if he wasn't leaning too far forward all over again.

"What do you care?" she groused back at him.

That was the problem between them. He'd always cared. After all this time, he still did. The sweep of her lashes on hollowed cheeks that used to be plump and full and pink from the sun caught his ire. Hell, he could feel her bony arms under his fingertips. She had no meat on her.

"What are you? Anorexic? Bulimic?" he asked instead of answering her question.

She rolled what he knew were the prettiest moss-green eyes on earth, even though he couldn't see their color in the dark. Jessie's eyes were always too big for her pretty face. They were always the wellspring of her truest emotions, too. A guy could look into them and see her soul all day long and still need more. She might lie and tell you she was okay, but the light in those eyes always gave her away. "No silly. I diet. All models do."

He stared down at her breasts, the ones that used to push against her shirt and make him want to do more than just catch a glimpse. They didn't seem as shrunken as the rest of her. "Let me guess. Silicone? Saline? Weren't the ones you were born with big enough?"

She wiggled to get away, jerking her arms up to break his hold. "You know what? You're still an ass. They're real, but I don't have to put up with this, this interrogation, not from you, not from anyone. The steers are home. It's late. Take your mare and thanks a heap for all your help."

She shouldn't have made being neighborly a thing of sarcasm. He held on tight to her arms and glared into her stormy depths, fighting the rising urgency springing to life in his body and soul. Storm. Her parents should've named her Storm. Then they'd be Storm and Smoke, and together they'd be lightning and thunder, and—

What the hell am I thinking?

Jess went perfectly still, the only sound was her heart pounding in the quiet night, hypnotizing him with her sudden change in direction. Intoxicating him. He didn't want to go home. Not like this.

With one hard hand, he claimed the nape of her stiff neck even as her palms went flat to the center of his chest, stopping him. Like she was big enough to try.

He leaned into her mouth despite the barrier between them, eyeing her reaction. No hint of fear shifted over her proud face, and damn it. She should be afraid. She, of all people, should be shaking in her fancy, high-heeled shoes. Men on several continents were afraid of him, yet there she stood, her shoulders squared. Her chin up. Daring him. Baiting him. Holding him at bay while she drew him in. Licking her lips and...

Oh, hell.

He crashed into her mouth, pinning her against the side of a nervous Tango, needing to teach Jess a lesson or two before the mare turned skittish and sidestepped for more space. "Steady girl," he murmured huskily, and he honestly didn't know which female he meant, the mare or the fiery filly at his fingertips.

Jess's arms came up easily from his chest to his neck, surrounding him in the cocoon of her breasts, the only lush part of her body—thank God they were real—and her warm lips. Her silky tangles.

Her chin bumped his. Her nose rubbed against his cheek. Her fingertips tunneled over his scalp and through his hair, lighting up every male receptor from his head to his toes. Jess scrubbed over his ears, his forehead, and his face like a blind woman, mapping her way in the dark.

When she nipped his bottom lip, he groaned, opening up to him before he pressed her for more, her tongue dancing over his lips and teeth. Tasting. Licking. Moaning with relish as if she hadn't eaten in days. He sure as hell hadn't. Not like this. Not in a damned long time.

God, he was hungry. He'd been outcast for too long, and this woman was manna fallen out of a clear night sky. He melted inside, his core gone hard but his heart glowing like Chernobyl. No woman had ever meant as much to him as Jess. Her open arms and the warmth of her slender body penetrated his last defense, a feminine arrow straight to his cold heart. It slithered past the granite walls he'd built, past every last coded barrier and secret combination a warrior knew. He couldn't block her if he tried.

Starved for the candy sweet taste of her mouth, he trapped her head in his wide palms, his thumbs under her trembling chin as he fed on the tender nectar of her willing lips. With every panting breath, the fire in her soul brought him back to life, the chocolate and orange taste on her tongue, his for the taking. Defiantly feminine yet gently submissive. Wild and sweet and spicy, full of heat. Full of sass.

He launched himself into the moist cavern of her back-talking mouth, plundering it with long demanding sweeps of his tongue. The appetite he'd suppressed too long for this woman and this woman alone, roared back to life with a vengeance. He licked her lips and nibbled and nipped, his craving morphing into fire crackling in his veins. There was no way to rein in his mouth any more than his heart. Smoke had to have her, all of her.

Gradually, his rage gave way to tenderness, his sins to redemption. He knew to his soul that this was what he needed. Who he wanted. Jess was faith, hope, and forgiveness, maybe even—love. A choke strangled at the back of his throat, welling up in his eyes, with her caught in the crook of his arm like she was. He'd missed this woman. He needed her heart. Her soul. Her love.

Shifting his stance to anchor them, he bent his head to wipe his eyes on his shoulder then suckled at her neck, so she'd never see how weak he was. Her breath caught the moment his mouth braced her skin, lighting the sizzle of another flash fire in his veins, a molten flow that begged release. She leaned back, granting more access to more skin, and with that gentle permission, his body hardened with urgency. An addiction for the pleasure of her mouth pooled deep in his groin, driving him to take her to her knees.

Here. Now. Under the wide Texas sky.

As they knelt together in the grass, her fingers shifted to his gut and from there to his belt buckle. A lightning strike like no other blasted through him. This woman was reading his mind.

The roar in his blood drowned out his last flicker of common sense. Fighting he understood, but not this tender exchange of body heat and hearts. Not this strong woman's matching appetite for him. Her welcoming response was the last thing he'd expected or deserved. It had been so long since anyone cared enough to get in his face. To stand up to him. To dare him to live.

Growling out of sheer feral need, he laid her down in the moist, dew laden grass. With one slice of his hand, her shirt buttons flew to who knew where, and his palm tested the weight of her breast still trapped in its silken cup. Lust for every last piece of her tender body roared through him. Smoke gave in and bowed his face, suckling her nipple through the silk, inhaling the heavenly warm scent of this luscious female in heat. Powdery. Flowery. His for the taking.

Whimpering, she arched into him, growling, holding him close with her fingernails clamped onto his scalp. He always knew it would be this way with this rowdy cowgirl. Push and shove. Give and take. But tonight was definitely a night for taking. The shirt had to go. Then the bra. At last she lay stripped to her waist, her body undulating with need. Her dewy eyes were still too big for her face. Her cheeks too gaunt. Breathing hard. Still licking her lips, a small smile tugged at the corners of her mouth.

He took a long time-out just to drink in the sight of her, now bared and blessed by midnight's silvery glow. Tenderly, he pushed her bra up and filled his palm with one luscious breast. The pad of his callused thumb scraped across her still wet nipple, tightening it into a knot that begged for more of his mouth. He lay there amazed that something so delicate as a woman's nipple could command a man the likes of him. The compulsion to pray overwhelmed Smoke. To give thanks to his Heavenly Father for not throwing him away like his earthly parents had. For this solitary moment of peace and reconnection to what mattered most.

"Don't you dare stop now, Smoke," she hissed, her gentle fingers stroking the muscles at his throat.

As if he could've stopped. He lowered his face into the valley between her breasts, his nostrils flared wide, committing the scent of her petal soft skin to his memory. Every last fragrant epithelial. Every last atom.

Like a cat, she rubbed her chin against his forehead, her nose in his hair. A sexy purr vibrated up from her throat, enticing him to finish the act and claim her. He could feel her throbbing pulse thrumming against his body, and he wanted her. No, he needed her.

Smoke covered that perfect mauve peak, drawing it into the moist heat of his mouth, forming a suction between man and woman. Sublime pleasure rippled up his spine at the dimension he'd lost himself in, somewhere between heaven and earth with no hell in sight for a blessed change.

He suckled strongly, needing to mark Jess as his, to brand her creamy skin with his bite marks and enough raspberries that all would know he'd been there. That he'd kill any who challenged him for her. That they were foolish to dare try.

Primitive instinct pounded through him, lighting him up. The elemental beast within charged to life. Possessively, he molded his mouth to the swell just above her right breast, the part of her that might show above her shirt. Biting her. Branding her. *Mine. All mine.*

She tugged him out of his shirt, tossing it over her head, while her hot fingertips mapped his muscular shoulders, molded the solid planes of his pecs, scratched over his ribs, and paused to pinch his flat, man nipples.

"You like to play rough, do you?" he growled into her breasts, now slick with the heady perfume of feminine sweat and desire.

"No," she murmured even as she raked her nails down his belly to his zipper. "I like to play for keeps."

That did it. He drew his tongue up between her breasts and on up to her mouth. The time had come for more than foreplay. With his heart in his throat, Smoke planted his elbows at each side of her head and glared down into her eyes. "Take your damned pants off, Jess."

CHAPTER EIGHT

She couldn't strip fast enough. Jessie arched her hips and dragged the capris down until it became too difficult to remove them. Smoke lost patience and jerked them off and away. By then he was just as naked, his jeans gone, and his eyes bright with animal need.

Jessie West, the woman every grasping model in the world, had a fully aroused male blanketing her body, a fierce warrior with thick black butterfly wings for lashes. A stubborn angular jaw. Clean black brows that seemed to have forgotten how not to frown. A barely dusted rock-solid chest, the muscles marred only by the dark ink of a half-skull over his heart, its top teeth long and dripping with black drops, maybe blood. A decorative crucifix tattooed on one massive bicep that all by itself screamed, *'Come get some. Dare try.'*

She dared. Who cared that she was naked in the grass beside a pasture of nosy longhorns? Who cared that she might soon be on her knees and screaming for more? She didn't. The only thought Jessie had was of putting a smile on this tormented man's face. And she knew how to do it, by making him grunt and groan and bellow with pleasure until he reached for the stars. Pleasing him until he knew damned sure he was loved and had not been forgotten. Wanton desire lapped at her core.

"I don't love you," he growled, his eyes graveyard black as he leaned over her, his massive forearms framing her head, one knee between her legs. His face was still lost in shadow and too many memories.

Like I believe that? Damn, this man was a liar.

"You're just saying that," she said sweetly and hotly, her fingers tunneling through the roots of his hair again. "You've loved me since we were kids, and I know it. You always will love me because you always have. You just won't let yourself admit it."

"No," he insisted with a groan that reached all the way to her womb, making her body weep with lust and tears and desire. "I don't. Never have. Never will."

Yeah right. Closing her eyes, Jessie swallowed hard at his way of keeping his pain in check. He'd proclaimed much too loud and with too much passion, but Jessie knew Smoke better than to believe his grumbly rejection now. He'd always been the stoic one, the toughest kid in the rodeo. The one who'd never showed emotions, whether he'd been stomped by antsy livestock or when he'd nailed that ten second ride. The one who forever denied that he cared what happened to Ethan's baby sister, when she knew darned well he did.

Her heart whispered to brush the ghosts off his wide, muscled shoulders, so he would finally be rid of the guilt he carried. So he'd be able to take in a deep, cleansing breath. She longed to kiss the sorrow out of his eyes and wash the mortal sins— whether perceived or real—off his soul. Maybe then, he'd see her for who she was and had always been. *His* woman.

Instead of pushing him away like he probably wanted, she cupped his jaw, her thumbs on this hard man's stubborn chin and her fingers in his hair as she pulled him to her nose. "Yes, you do love me, my sweet, sweet boy. You won't admit it because you're afraid you'll get hurt again, but I know better. It's okay with me if you can't say it yet. I don't need words. I just need you." *I always have.*

He growled a throaty denial, but she didn't believe that either, not with the tenderness welling up in his black eyes, the same tender light from all those years ago. Not with him paused at her feminine doorway to forever. Where inches counted. Where no man had been before. That singular, sacred, intimate place where one nudge forward would bind her to him from this night on—if he were brave enough.

"It's not okay," he ground out even as the spark in his eye mellowed.

Whatever that meant. She'd forgotten what she'd asked or said. He sounded so lost. So incredibly alone. Jessie reached one fingertip to the sharp point of his spiked black brow. This man never smiled, and if she hadn't known Smoke better, she would've thought him cold and brutal. But that was just a mask, his way of dealing with the betrayal his parents put him through. The instant her fingertip met his skin, he reminded her of a stray dog that had been kicked, yelled at, and slapped until it traded the risk of genuine human contact for solitude and safety.

Smoke was that dog. He'd seen so much in his life. Done so much. It must haunt him. Never give him peace. Never let him rest. He was that tormented wanderer without a place to come home to at the end of a day. Cast out by the two people who should've loved him unconditionally. Exiled. The unworthy and despised son who believed himself unlovable. Damn it, what his parents did was wrong.

It was a despicable fate they'd consigned him to, this noble hero who'd fought with honor for his country, to have been told to never come home again. That he was a murderer and dead to them. What were they thinking?

Jessie's heart ached to be that one soft landing place in a world gone heartless and cold. Spreading her knees, she opened her body and her soul to him. His hips settled where he desperately needed to be. And there he lay, his bare belly to hers, his back arched on the verge of doing something wonderfully wicked instead of sinfully wrong. On the edge of eternity instead of insanity.

"I do love you," she murmured, never taking her eyes off him.

Angrily, he thrust forward and speared her like he meant to teach her a lesson when he was the one desperately in need of knowledge. Of learning about love and life and laughter.

It didn't hurt. Honest. He hadn't gone in deep enough to hurt her. Not yet. It just took a moment to get used to the length and width of him being inside of her body, where miracles could still happen. Before he could punctuate that lesson with his version of an exclamation point by impaling her, Jessie gave him the gift she'd waited a lifetime to say.

"I'm a virgin, Smoke Montoya." Her voice caught, tears springing to her eyes. She'd loved him for so long. "I've waited for you, and tonight... I'm all yours."

His head reared back, his face shadowed with darkness that took her breath. "You're what?" he barked. "A... My God, you're a what?"

Please don't be mad about that, too. "A virgin," she whispered, her fingertips light on his cheeks, her resolve trembling. Had she waited for nothing? Would this be the final betrayal that pushed him away forever? "You're my first true love, and my only."

"Shit! Why didn't you say something before?" he ground out, his tense body on rigid hold, the tip of his manhood pulsing hot and heavy at the slippery cusp of forever. At least that part of his body was still plenty happy to see her.

Jessie cupped his face with both hands, nervously needing him to take that plunge with her—into her—and to never let her go. To need her more than he needed his anger.

"But I..." His breath hitched as a shudder stalked up his body. "Why didn't you tell me? Did I... did I hurt you?" he asked earnestly, peering closer with that black savage gaze he did so well. It alone was enough to frighten her off, but ah! This wild man was breaking her heart.

She tilted her chin into his, and, tugging him to her mouth, she kissed his soft lips gently and carefully, wanting him to feel what was in her heart before he turned sullen and threw her gift away. "I needed to come home so I could tell you face to face. I love you, Smoke, and I've waited for you. You didn't hurt me. Nothing you've ever said or done could hurt me, because I know who you really are. I see you."

"Bullshit!" The pain snapped out of him. Too easily, she could read the flare of anger in his eyes.

The indecision. The arrogant dare that he could hurt her, and he knew it. That part of him wanted her to pay. "You knew I'd be here? What'd you do, talk to Betty?"

See? There he was again, ready to strike before someone hurt him. The Navy had taught him well.

Jessie shook her head. "No. I'm so sorry, Smoke. But I didn't realize you'd lost your parents until I arrived at your place tonight, but..." And there she stopped. As bad as she felt for all he'd lost, there was no sense explaining the string of coincidence that had brought them to this singular decision point. She'd already bared her heart and her body for the taking or the breaking.

Now it was his turn. He needed to want her, too. He needed to remember the good times between them, that all was not lost. That his parents were the ones who'd given up on him, not her.

The change happened slowly. The tight grip of his fingers on her ass softened. The light finally came on, a tender brightening down deep in the moody core of his inky, black pupils. A long troubled sigh breathed out of him in one ragged exhale. He touched his nose to hers. "I don't deserve you," he whispered sorrowfully. "Someone else. Anyone else. Not me."

Jessie heard goodbye in his words. She was losing him. She wrapped her arms around his strong, stiff neck and held on tightly, smothering his face to her breasts where he belonged. Tears brimmed as she drew the scent of his clean hair into her soul, the fresh scent of soap and leather, of horses and this one-in-a-million, wild Texas night. There could never be another so rare, and it would kill her if he rejected her now.

His lips melded a fiery kiss between her breasts. A goodbye kiss.

No, no. No.

A ragged sob hiccupped out of her. Jessie swallowed hard. She of all people had rejection coming. A woman can only reap what she'd sown, and Jessie had sown nothing but distance with her own selfish superiority. Not once had she written Smoke, and she knew now that all her excuses were dust in the wind. She should've written. She should've called. She should've told him long ago she loved him. Only him. *Always him...*

Ethan had left, though not of his own volition, but gone was gone. Why should she expect anything different from the universe than a rebuff from the man she loved? Than to live a bitter rich life all by her rich bitch self?

Jessie held her breath, willing to beg, her tears brimming, and the universe on hold. "Please don't go, Smoke. Don't leave me again."

He lifted his head out of her tangled embrace, but just enough to glare at her. "If I remember right, you were the one who left Ethan and me. You had to be a princess, so off you went to New York City."

Her fingernails dug deeper into his shoulders muscles. He was right. This was her fault. The little girl in her cried out for all of her wicked, thoughtless, past mistakes. "I know, and I'm sorry, but I... God, I was just a kid. Don't go—"

Ah! He took her by surprise. With one decisive thrust of his hips, the seal was broken, and, *oh, my God.* He was—in. And he was hot and big and too rough and...

Oh my, yes. She blinked the pinch of virginal pain away as her body adjusted to its new reality and accepted his unexpected gift. A silent sob climbed up her throat at the intimacy and the sting of suddenly sharing the same skin with the only man she truly loved.

Smoke bumped his scruffy chin to her nose before he covered her mouth with his. This time around, it was infinitely soft and gentle, a searing smoky weld that tugged at her heartstrings, forging them—for the moment— into one. "Who said anything about leaving?"

Chapter Nine

There under the wide Texas sky, Smoke pummeled her sweet body with his until every last star fell to earth around them. Until they made their own brand of fireworks. Jess's lush, warm sweet body was a welcome home he never wanted to leave. When she soared heavenward and came, writhing against him in womanly strength and fervor, her most secret places suckled him as strong as he'd suckled at her breast. He clenched her narrow ass, holding her still while he plunged deeper and came home again. And again. She came with him every single time.

And still, he wanted more.

This was what he'd been searching for these last desperate years, this one sweet, stubborn woman with forever in her eyes. The one who'd been with him through childhood heartache, adolescent ups and downs, the aftermath of all those fights with his dad, and every single spill during their crazy-fun rodeos.

He wasn't smart enough to know then why she'd given up barrel racing for beauty pageants, but he should've guessed. He'd had plenty of time to think about it since then.

Jess's mom had gotten her into her first beauty pageant. It was a mother and daughter bonding time like no other. For the first time, Jess wore dresses instead of jeans. She had her hair fixed. She primped for Ethan and him. When she blushed, his heart raced. The age difference was always their problem. She was a kid and his best buddy's little sister. Love seemed like sacrilege. The lust, too.

But then everything changed. Within weeks of that first pageant crown and her dazzling success, Jess and Ethan's mom and dad were killed in a car accident. Smoke was eighteen and fighting with his old man day-in and day-out, too angry and awkward to know what emotional support a grieving fourteen-year-old girl needed.

He turned to the Navy and a way out of his nightmare at home.

Jess turned to the one thing she had left of her mother, those damned pageants. He went one way, she the other. Each pageant pulled her farther from her childhood and eventually her brother. After she won Miss Texas, New York sat up and took notice, and then, took her.

Smoke was proud of Jess's accomplishments, but by then he was on his way to Basic Underwater Demolition, BUDs. He'd learned to earn his trident every day, and she learned about fame and fortune. They weren't more than childhood friends anyway. Certainly not lovers. Not even boyfriend and girlfriend. They were just two kids who'd lived on the same dirt road and happened to like rodeo.

Each of them had gone in search of their own brand of survival. He'd learned the hard man's ways. The ways of the SEAL. The warrior code. She'd learned to be something she wasn't. An industry icon. Just another pretty face. Both of them had ended up alone and miserable. What the hell were they thinking?

He sunk his face into the warm crook of her neck, wanting that elusive comfort she'd so vigorously offered. Was any of this real? After all this time, could it be so easy? Could this tender moment last?

The wild woman in his arms made him strong even when she took every last bit of his strength and his will, but he remembered that stubborn, mouthy girl-child he'd fallen in love with. Back then, no one could make him angrier, but at the same time, no one got him like Jessie West. One smile. One touch. And there he was again, an older boy falling for a mature and sensitive twelve-year-old girl who'd told him to get off the ground and back on that bucking bronco. That sure, he could do it. That he had to get his ass back in that saddle or he'd never ride again. That he'd be a wimp the rest of his life if he didn't. That she knew he could do it.

Damned if that bossy little girl wasn't the one who'd made him the man he was today. He nibbled a trail up her shivering neck to her ticklish ear. The night was dark and made for making love, for the tenderest of ecstasies, for wanton sex with that one-in-a-million gentle woman who had her own share of demons.

"What say we take this rodeo inside?" he asked hotly, his tongue running along the satin curl of her ear.

"Mmm, yes, please," she murmured, her lashes lowered, her breath as soft as angel wings on his collarbone.

Like Adam with Eve, Smoke lifted his bare-naked lady into the shelter of his arms and carried her trembling body up the steps and into her home. She locked her long legs around his waist, her head bumping beneath his chin. He hadn't felt so powerful or so physically strong in years. Or this sure.

The West home had been built in the seventies. Older. Narrower. Smaller rooms and still smaller bathrooms, but large enough for what he had planned. He just didn't expect to be greeted by a bundle of pompoms on steroids nor the cold wet goose on his rear.

"What the hell's that?" he growled, tucking his ass in while keeping an eye on the big white dog with the whip of a tail and a big, fluffy cotton ball at the end of it.

Jess giggled. "That's Fluffy. My poodle. Be nice to him."

"Looks like he got caught between a twister and a hair dryer. Gawd. He's got ribbons in his ears. What'd you do to him? Turn him into a female?"

She giggled again. "Yes, he's neutered, but he likes ribbons. He's a standard poodle. Fluffy's supposed to look like that."

Smoke growled. "No guy-dog likes sissy ribbons, and what kind of a name is Fluffy? What's wrong with Spike?" He managed one quick pat to Fluffy's cottony head before he continued through the house. "Still the bedroom on the right?" he asked while he angled her headfirst through the narrow hall, then shut the bedroom door to keep the dog out.

Smoke had been in this house before, in her bedroom too, but never as her lover. Only as her brother's trustworthy friend. The one in the background when tragedy came calling and stole her parents. The silent guy in the shadows when his best girlfriend impulsively and launched her shattered heart and lost soul into the insane world of pageants, all because she couldn't bear the loss of her mother. The guy who wasn't man enough to tell her to get her butt back in the saddle for a change. That he knew she was stronger than her heartache. That he had her back. The fool who'd carved her initials inside a heart on a stupid tree.

That guy.

"Yes," she murmured breathily, her arms circling his shoulders and her lips tracing liquid fire up his neck. Tickling that sweet spot under his chin. Making him shiver.

Gently, he dropped one knee to her bed and leaned her onto her pillow. Funny. Ethan hadn't changed a thing in her room. That goofy pink lava lamp still glowed in the corner under a poster of Jimmy Star, a local PRCA bull-rider from years ago.

"Still keeping track of Rodeo Hall of Famers?" he grumbled, an irrational spike of jealousy rippling up his spine at the thought of Jess looking at another man before she fell asleep at night.

"Still keeping track of prime man flesh," she had the audacity to reply. *The tease.*

"Man flesh, huh?" he asked as he nudged her legs apart with his knee and leaned in to pick up where they'd left off. "There'd better just be one man's flesh in that scenario," he breathed threateningly into the hollow of her neck before. "And it better be me."

Bucking up from the bed, she toppled him onto his back, his head now on her pillow and her nose crinkled with sexy mischief. A dark veil of ebony silk descended around his face, and he was lost inside their very own sensual world where the borders of their bodies faded into each other. Where the silken strands of her hair merged with the short black of his. Where she butted up against him. Literally. The cheeks of her sweet ass nestled over his thighs, her legs spread wide as her core whispered hot lovely temptation to a very hungry man.

Tightening his palm around the nape of her neck, he pulled her down into his face, loving the sway of her breasts before her nipples peaked hard and ready over his chest. Tracing her bottom lip with his index finger, he tried to remember what they'd been fighting about. Nothing seemed important now except playing with this woman's sexy body and tasting every last honey-drenched fold. Making damned sure she was sore—but happy—in the morning.

"You want me?" she asked, that sexy chin jutted forward in her own version of female persuasion. Like he needed persuading.

Smoke flexed his hips and instantly found the secret slick, hiding place that now belonged to him. Where only he'd been. In the universe of all imaginable possibilities, he'd never once realized how much that simple gift of feminine purity meant, not after all the vile things he'd seen during his military life, and the desperate places he'd been. He surely didn't deserve the gift, but it was his. He'd claimed what she offered, what she'd held back from others and saved just for him.

Honored the world over, innocence and virginity were still bought by powerful men and sold to highest bidders in more countries than he wanted to think about. But here, in this tiny throwback bedroom from another decade, when teenaged rodeo-wannabes ruled the world—or thought they did—there rode the rodeo queen of his world. Offering her body and her heart. And he was her steed. Her very humble steed.

An odd sensation in his chest tightened around his heart. Love. He let it roll through him. Let it work its wonderful, squeezing, magnificent magic.

Her hard-to-work-with-diva rep made sense now. Of course the media called her a bitch. She didn't fit in the modeling world that immersed itself in the murky depths of porn and all its twisted vagaries. The runways of the industry were rife with addictions for more and more skin, yet she'd risen through the ranks, an unlikely meteor of moral standards. The easiest way to make enemies was to stand out from the crowd. Be different. Be better. Stay pure and stay true.

He'd never doubted her. Not once. Despite the body-conscious world she worked and thrived in, Jessie West wasn't one to lie. Yes, she might have posed as her assistant in a poor attempt at anonymity, but there was no cruelty or underhandedness to her ill-fated scheme. Just reverence for the brother she'd loved. Just the desire to return home, and for one moment, be the little kid she used to be, the adoring baby sister.

Smoke held her gaze, commanding her with his wide manly palms to make that womanly ass move. To play and tease and come again—just for him.

A sultry smile shone down on him as she tipped forward, her core positioned greedily over him, her breasts mashed against his chest, and her lips melded to his. He clenched that skinny backside. One thrust was all it took, and they were on their way again. It didn't take long to climb that staircase to the stars, to claim each other with grinding bodies and quivering screams that no one else had the right to hear, not even the longhorns.

The duty to care for his father's horses still standing in her backyard with their saddles on, niggled at the extreme recesses of Smoke's mind. Chip and Tango needed to be brushed down, watered and fed, but not now. He wouldn't forget them, but first, he needed to finish this ride for the delectable lady cowboy straddling him. He needed to claim her until—the cows came home.

"Oh. Oh. Oh!" she squealed, rocking hard and tight and wet against him, her fingers splayed on his chest, her hair a shimmering midnight veil of rippling ebony waves. "There. Right there. Oh, please. Don't stop," she ground out, locked in a rhythm as old as time, her pretty eyes closed in fierce concentration of the upcoming—coming.

He cupped her hips and let her ride, his thumbs snug in the creases at her groin. His fingers splayed over her hipbones, holding her steady as her fifth orgasm zipped up her spine, arced through her body, and took control. Of course, he'd counted. He was a man.

From deep inside, every last feminine muscle clenched, bearing down on him, crushing his thighs in a death grip only a woman in the throes of passion could achieve. Blowing on her still moist nipples sent another shiver coursing up her belly, tightening her grip on him again.

He could play her body like this all night.

Goosebumps lifted up from her skin, so he sent another heated breath over her naked self, loving the automatic feminine impulse to squeeze. Smoke slowed his pace, giving her time to enjoy the aftershocks before he took her hard again. Holding her hips fast, he didn't let her catch her breath before they flew again. He soared with her, encased so deep inside her velvety warmth he never wanted to leave. For those mind shattering seconds, he was free of ghosts and regrets and bitterness. He was himself again, a kid in love with the most beautiful girl in the world. He was free. Redemption was real. Forgiveness, too.

They fell from the stars together. Slowly, like lazy sparks from dazzling fireworks. Connected forever, even as the world came back into view around them. Sheets. Pillows. The soft pink glow of bubbling melted wax. Some loser named Jimmy Star.

"Ah, ah," she ground out, panting her sweet hot breath in his face, and blowing strands of hair out of her mouth as she sought after every last inch of pleasure, grinding against him, bone to bone and heart to heart. "Why didn't we do this years ago? It feels so goooooooood."

He couldn't help it. He groaned at the excited tremor and the pleasure in her hoarse voice. "You were too young." *Silly, beautiful girl.* "I was eighteen when I left home. You were fourteen. I don't think folks would've understood us having sex back then."

A grin cracked over her face. "Oh, yeah, I was just a kid, huh?"

"But you were already going places, Jess. You were born to be a star." He smoothed the loose tangles of her hair away from her face and tugged her forward for another soft kiss on her lips. And Smoke Montoya did something he hadn't done in years.

He smiled.

CHAPTER TEN

"So, umm, what do you want to do now?" Jessie asked the handsome guy sprawled alongside her on the double bed in her childhood room where her biggest dream had finally come true.

They'd crawled under the sheets after having the most fantastic sex ever. Afterwards, Smoke left to tend to his horses, but he returned quickly, his bare feet damp and cold from the dew-drenched lawn. They'd snuggled like two little kids. Then he'd fallen asleep on his back, with her tucked in tight under one arm, his other draped over his eyes. This morning, the sheet lay over their hips, leaving them bare from the waist up.

"I don't know about you, but I was thinking breakfast," he grumbled, his sexy voice beneath under her fingertips. "I've got sandwiches, cupcakes, and coffee at my place, if you don't want to cook."

Using just the tip of her tongue to entice him, she trailed a moist edge along his neck to his ear. "What's this *if* I don't want to cook business? Don't you know how to grill bacon?" she breathed, thrilled when her touch raised goose bumps on his bare belly. The man had a seriously carved set of abdominals.

She'd spent the last half hour watching him sleep, recalling every line and edge to his manly face, counting his breaths, and timing his pulse, the soft beats at the hollow of his deeply tanned neck. Just listening to him breathe. Okay, so she'd also been licking her lips, dying for him to wake up, roll over, and make love to her again, too. But mostly, she'd just watched him, remembering the boy she'd once known and memorizing the man relaxed beside her now.

He was all male, his edges hard and sharp. The tattooed skull on his chest, with its dripping, elongated fangs, declared him a warrior. The brackets at the corners of his full lips were carved deep and unsmiling. Rays etched out from the corners of his eyes, but they weren't laugh lines. Something crueler. More intense. A darkness shadowed him until he'd smiled last night. For a moment, the happy cowboy she used to know glimmered through the rough Navy SEAL camouflage. Smoke was still in there. Somewhere. He was just different. No longer the innocent boy.

Feeling the urge to trap him into another round of hot, heavy sex, she eased her fingertips over his taut six-pack and let her fingers do the walking to man-land. He moved fast. Flattening her hand to his belly, he tugged her fingers to his lips and nipped her knuckle. "You don't give a guy much time to recuperate, do you?"

"What? Are you tired?" she teased, blowing a breath over his hair-roughened pecs, making his nipples perk up. "A big guy like you?"

"Not hardly." With a grunt, he had her on her back again, nose to nose and his breath in her face. Her hands were trapped over her head, the perfect position for kickoff, but she didn't see the winning game of a quarterback in his eyes. Only worry and questions. His hair hung over brooding eyes. "What are we doing here, Jess? Is any of this real? You said you play for keeps. What'd that mean?"

Oh, Smoke, my incredibly handsome lost boy. Loosening the shackle of his hands, she ran her fingers into his hair and over his head, clutching him tight, nose-to-nose. "After all we've done to each other, now you're worried?"

"Yes," he said softly, his tone not wavering as he licked the tip of her nose. "Things happen. People change. Even playing-for-keeps rules change."

It was no wonder he doubted. The biggest rule of all time, the supposedly binding love between parents and their only child, had changed him. Then Jessie had deserted him, too, just like his parents. In a way. Was there anyone besides the guys on his SEAL team who hadn't betrayed him? She couldn't dredge up one name of a past friend or date. The only ones he'd been close to growing up were Ethan and her. She'd never meant to hurt him, but she had. Damn.

"It means I think you're right. Part of me came home for selfish reasons, but now that I'm here, I don't want to go back to New York. I want to stay in bed with you for the rest of my life." She hooked her arms around his strong neck, determined to seduce him if he'd let her. "I want you, Smoke. Just you. Can't we stay like this forever?"

The darkness in his eyes softened. The harsh worry lines at his brows faded. Relaxing his heavier body, he pinned her solidly to the mattress. "But you're right. You have obligations. I read the papers. I've seen the drama play out, when powerful people don't get their way. The court battles. You said you've got an agent. Won't he have something to say about your quitting?"

She nodded, savoring the masculine sensation of her man's body lying on hers. The hair-roughened legs between her thighs. The heat of velvet steel on her stomach. "Fernando Sonoma. Yes. Ethan hired him. He wanted the best manager for me, someone who could make me a star."

Smoke jerked back enough to look down at her, his brows knitted. "You're kidding me? Fernando Sonoma, as in the Sonoma brothers, as in the Sonoma cartel out of Mexico? No wonder you're a big hit."

"Excuse me?" Jessie smacked that warm muscled wall at her fingertips. "I'll have you know I'm very good at my job. Everybody wants to be me."

Smoke set her straight, his elbows beside her shoulders and his hands framing her head. "No, they don't. And I didn't mean you weren't good at what you do, baby. Of course you're good. Look at you. You're hot damned sexy and you're smart, but did Ethan know this Fernando dude was tangled up with the cartel when he hired him?" Smoke traced her bottom lip with his fingertip, melting her willpower even as he interrogated her.

"Uh-uh," Jessie murmured, glad to finally have someone she could to talk with about the mess she was in. She hadn't even minded him calling her baby. He meant it as an honest endearment, not the smutty come-on most other guys intended. "And now Fernando wants me to sign up for the Playboy shoot. The swimsuit edition in Cannes was his idea. He keeps pushing, and so far, he's listened to my objections. But every time I turn around, he wants a little more submission and fewer clothes. The next thing you know, I'll be posing nude."

"Like hell you will," Smoke growled, his white teeth bared like a wolf's. "No one gets to see your naked ass but me."

She would've giggled, but all this talk about business and the headaches that came with it, drained the romance out of her. Jessie snuggled in under Smoke's bristly chin, loving the manly scrape at her forehead and the clean, crisp scent of his skin. "I've decided. I'm quitting my modeling career," she whispered into his neck. "I'll call Fernando today to see what I have to do."

"No, Jess. Don't call your agent. You'll call a lawyer to find out what it'll take to get out of your contract. I doubt it'll be easy, and you need to be ready to swing back if Sonoma plays hardball. A guy like him isn't going to be happy. He won't take your quitting lying down. You might not get out of this contract without a log, drawn out court battle. Do you have a copy of it with you?"

"I can get one. It's not all adventure and glamour, you know. Modeling," she sighed. "I've worked hard, but in the back of my mind, I always felt like maybe I had my ladder up against the wrong tree. Like I had what I thought I wanted, only I didn't. Not really. Does that make sense?"

Smoke lifted a thick chunk of her hair and held it to his nose, sniffing the sleek curl as he let it wind over his thumb. A comfortable male growl rumbled under her ear. "I'm glad you came home, Jess."

"Does that mean you're staying, too?" she asked hopefully.

"I don't know. Right now, it just means I'm glad we're both here at the same time."

"Smoke?" she asked, wishing he'd tell her he loved her. "What do you want for breakfast?"

"Silly girl," he growled as he lifted to his knees, and took her with him. Rolling her over, he shifted his weight down her delectable body, his tongue slick and warm on her belly button. "I'm having you."

CHAPTER ELEVEN

"Who's pounding on my door?" Rolling to her feet, Jessie grabbed her fluffy pink bathrobe. Out of her closet.

"Don't answer it," Smoke grumbled, his arm stretched out to haul her back under the sheets. "Whoever it is, they can go away."

"It's okay. I'll be right back. If you're good, I might bring you a cup of coffee. Cream and sugar like before?"

"Woman, I'm always good." His morning voice was still growly deep after another long get together. "Black's better."

She had to look twice. Damn. He was a long-legged sight for sore eyes, all stretched out, his feet well past the end of her bed, the sheet barely covering his hips. She bit her bottom lip, not sure she cared who was at her door. She had a tiger in her bed, a sexy, lithe tiger with scruffy pecs and a dark line pointing the way to what lay—make that stood—beneath the sheet and was obviously very happy to see her.

The darkest, deep brown eyes scorched her, but the best part? She cocked her head, her hand on her hip, and a skip in her heart. Like a lovesick teenager, she had to tell Smoke in case he didn't know. "You're smiling again."

This was so not the same fierce guy who'd all but mauled her last night under the stars.

He winked, a definite smolder tweaking the corners of his eyes and his lips. "It's been known to happen."

That made her smile, too. Her body ached in the most delightful places and this was a brand-new day. Yes, she had a hard task ahead dealing with Ethan's funeral services and getting away from the clutches of New York City. But things *were* going to work out, and Smoke *was* going to tell her he loved her, damn it. Soon. Really soon.

Padding barefoot through her living room, she shoved both hands through her thick hair and pushed it over her shoulders. She and her trusty companion, Fluffy, who'd been trained to greet her guests, opened her front door together.

"Can I help you?" she asked the silver-haired man in the slate-gray business suit standing on her porch, while Fluffy took his usual post at her feet.

"You most certainly can!" The enthusiastic guy stuck one hand forward and very nearly in her face. "I'm here to make you rich, little girl, and to turn Sunnyvale into the biggest tourist destination this side of the state. Name's Jenkins Lassiter. Pleased to meet you, ma'am. And you are...?"

Not a little girl...

Annoyed at his demeaning comment, Jessie crossed one arm over her chest to make sure her robe stayed closed, while she accepted the handshake. "Barbara Esposito," she lied, giving his hand back as quickly as possible. For a pushy salesman, she'd expected a stronger, more athletic grip, not the sweaty, limp noodle that left her fingers feeling like she needed to hurry and wash him off.

But when Fluffy grumbled a warning, that was enough for Jessie. People tended to discount her dog's intelligence because of his breed. Standard poodles weren't commonly used security dogs, and their puffy haircuts fooled most fans. But he wasn't a dog to mess with, and if he detected something that she couldn't, well, Fluffy's opinion of this creepy guy was good enough for her. She'd learned early that when he didn't like someone, he was usually right. Besides, she sensed it, too. Something was very off about Jenkins Lassiter.

Jess took a half step back, her hand on her doorknob. "It's too early for salesmen. What exactly do you want?"

He dipped his head, his sharp eyes scrolling to the large dog at her side, then quickly back to her. Still smiling that insincere I'm-only-here-because-I-want-something-from-you snake-oil-salesman grin. "You mind if I come in? This is important. It might take a while to explain it to you."

To me, huh?

Again, he'd seen her as a brainless, simpering female, someone he could walk over to get what he wanted. Well, guess again. After surviving New York City and the world of high fashion, she knew his kind all too well. "Whatever you're selling, I'm not interested."

Jessie didn't need to see him to know that Smoke was suddenly behind her, and that he was angry. "You heard the lady," he growled, his much larger hand engulfing hers on the knob. "Move on."

A satisfied bloom unfurled in the pit of her stomach. She liked the sound of the *you heard the lady*' that rolled so easily off his lips. He was going to say those other three little words real soon. She could feel it in her bones.

"What I'm selling is opportunity, young man," Lassiter declared boldly, that phony smile he'd pasted on his face not slipping a bit. "I'm here to make the homeowner of this valuable property a one-time good deal. I'm never wrong, and all of this" —he gestured broadly to the wide-open pasture behind him— "will soon be the site of the Blackland Prairie Casino. Just you kids wait and see. It'll be a destination resort, complete with a five-star hotel, an eighteen-hole golf course, a two hundred pad RV park with fifty-watt hook-ups, and seven, count 'em seven, fine restaurants. If you're smart, I'll make you a one-time good deal and let you invest at ground level. You'll be richer than any of your lazy neighbors Think about it." His brittle gaze zeroed back to her. "You are Jessie West, the famous model, aren't you? Why are you hiding in this slum?"

Her hackles lifted under that fluffy robe. The West Ranch was no slum, and how'd he even know who she was? But worse, he'd slammed the people she loved with that *lazy neighbors'* dig. Who did he think he was?

Before she could open her mouth to tell him to pound sand, Lassiter waved one hand dismissively, as if any reply from her was inconsequential. "No need to answer. I do my homework before I do business." His silvery brows furrowed as he cast a glance over his shoulder to the field of grazing bovines. "I know exactly who you are, Miss West, and how much you currently owe the bank. Right now, you own your penthouse in New York out right, but you're stuck with these eighty acres. If I'm not mistaken—and I'm not—you also own a seventeen-year loan on this worthless parcel. Six-percent interest. Your brother had less than fourteen thousand in his savings account, and he owned a maxed-out credit card with nine and a half percent. Same bank. Zero available credit and not a cent of it liquid. Whatever he spent his money on, it sure wasn't home improvement. This place has no curb appeal. I hate to be the one to say this, but your brother was a fool. Do I need to go on?"

His pretentious insult stiffened her spine. Ethan was no fool, Goddamnit. He was a dreamer, but now Jessie was pissed off, too. Because this money-grubbing creep was right. She now owned the West Ranch, most of it in grass hay, that, until just days ago, Ethan had divided between feeding his longhorn hobby during the winter and selling what hay he couldn't use, to local buyers in the summer. It wasn't much, but it had augmented his income from his job at the feed store in Sunnyvale.

The large red barn to the east was hers. It stored the hay and farming equipment, Ethan's and the bank's John Deere tractor. A rake. Plows. An ancient hay baler that had seen better days. Miscellaneous other farming machinery.

But those longhorns on the hoof were the real money. She hadn't yet had time to thoroughly study Ethan's pedigree records to validate his claim of elite Texas longhorn genetics. But if he was right, each one of those pesky critters chewing their cud out there in the early morning Texas sun, could fetch as much as one hundred thousand dollars at auction. Each.

That was what Ethan had spent the second mortgage on. And she, as Ethan's sole survivor and beneficiary, now owned thirty-six of those babies. Who would've thought that tough, rangy cattle would one day become a rich man's hobby? Apparently not Mr. Smartie-Pants Lassiter.

Smoke angled his wide shoulders, blocking Fluffy as he stepped to Jessie's side, his hand snaking around her waist and pulling her protectively into his hip. "What you need to do, Mr. Lassiter," he said evenly, his voice low and deliberate, "is get off Miss West's porch like she told you to. Leave your calling card. She'll call if she's interested. If she's not, you'll get over it. Now isn't the time for real estate offers. Maybe later."

Maybe never.

Lassiter grunted, his gaze dipping to Jessie's bare feet and edging deliberately up and over her early morning attire to her face, ending at her messy, I-just-had-the-most-amazing-sex-ever hair. "Hmmm. Yes, I can see she's" —he paused— "...truly grieving the loss of her only brother."

That did it. She rolled her neck, pissed at his continual insinuations. What the hell did he know? "I don't need your card, Lassiter. This is family land. It's been West property for three generations. I'm not selling. Goodbye, and don't bother coming back."

She should've slammed the door in his face, but common courtesy dictated otherwise, so she hesitated, giving him the last chance to say one decent thing. Just one. Maybe something like '*I'm sorry for your loss. Good day, ma'am.*'

But instead of backing off or doing the honorable thing, this slimy snake in the grass slid his hand into an inner suit pocket and produced a business card, which he promptly stuck in Smoke's face. "How about you, Mr. Montoya? Obviously, you're the smart one. That's your place west of here. Everyone knows you only came back to bury your folks, parents you haven't seen in what, four years? Are you interested in letting those two hundred eighteen acres go? You're a former Navy SEAL, unemployed and shiftless, right? I imagine you've got better things to do than hang around here and raise a couple old nags that should've been turned into dogfood years ago." He cocked his head like he thought he could read Smoke's mind. "What do you say? Interested? I can make it worth your while."

Oh, oh. Storm warning. Tornado alert. Run for cover. Another lethal F5 was on its way.

Smoke just went deadly still.

Jessie stopped breathing. Before Smoke could react—which wouldn't be pretty—she closed the door on Mr. Dumbass Jenkins Lassiter's arrogant face and turned on Smoke. "What a jerk," she hissed, her palms in the middle of his hard chest, needing to get his attention on her before he reopened her door and kicked Lassiter's ass out of the county. "Can you believe that creep? He's got a lot of nerve."

Smoke stared at the closed door, not moving, his fists clenched at his sides.

"Ethan bought a new coffeemaker," she rambled on her way to the kitchen, hoping Smoke would follow. "And he's got a dozen different flavors of gourmet coffee. Come pick your poison."

Yes, she wanted to smack Lassiter herself, but men like him weren't worth the trouble. He was just pushy like Fernando Sonoma, a shark and an opportunist by any other name.

"I've got coconut creamer," she called out. "Oh, wait. You like it black." *And you'd better not let that stupid guy get to you, not after the wonderful night we just shared.* "Are you coming? I've got bacon."

She could've slapped herself for that one. *Bacon? Really? Damn, he isn't a dog.* But it did get Fluffy's attention. Until then, he'd been standing at

Smoke's feet. Both of them stared at the door, Fluffy with his ears perked up, his head cocked as if listening, Smoke with his shoulders tight.

At last Fluffy gave up his post and joined her. Jessie ran her hand lovingly over her dog's puffy head, but her instincts were still on high alert. Pushy salesmen were not honest brokers. She had a feeling she hadn't seen the last of Jenkins Lassiter.

At last, Smoke stretched. He rolled one shoulder and turned her way.

She held out one hand, beckoning him to join her. The need to see him smile again clawed at her. She'd never felt so loved as last night in his arms. *Please don't let some real estate agent from hell ruin what we've got. Please.* "I'll fix breakfast. Promise I won't burn it."

Smoke ran a hand up the back of his neck, his expression dark and troubled. "I'm not hungry. Get dressed, Jess. We're going riding."

CHAPTER TWELVE

What made Smoke's mood worse was the flyer that son-of-a-bitchin' Lassiter stuck to Jess's door before he'd left, the same flyer Smoke found tacked to his tree. At first blush, it was simple marketing. Only this time Lassiter had added a hand scrawled: *You'll be sorry!*

What the hell did that mean? Was it an incentive or a threat? Lassiter knew damned well that Jess and Smoke were reeling from their losses. What kind of man, no matter how opportunistic, stooped so low? Apparently one with two last names.

Smoke wasn't really surprised at the intel the guy had on him or Jess. Real estate agents were nosy like that. They took advantage of people down on their luck. If anything, Lassiter' scathingly direct approach just might've solved Smoke's problems. As poorly timed as it was, the offer of a fast-sale and money in the bank still solved the problem of what to do with his parents' ranch. *The Lost Chaparral* would be sold and the horses auctioned off. Chip, Tango, and the mares could soon be grazing on someone else's ranch. Jasper and Minks, too.

But Jess? That was where the rubber hit the road. For the first time since he'd heard his parents were gone, Smoke was seriously conflicted about his future. Roaming Southeast Asia for the rest of his life felt dishonest. Cowardly. And selling Chip and the mares felt an awful lot like the worst kind of betrayal.

What sort of a man auctions off the four-legged brother he grew up with? Who'd care for gentle Tango, the other mares and the two stubborn mules as good as Caleb had? As good as Smoke would? He doubted new owners would give them carrots every day and a candied apple on

Christmas. Who'd make sure they were brushed down and currycombed after a sweaty run?

Horses and mules were no more than livestock to most ranchers. A commodity to be traded and bartered. But to Smoke? They were family.

Then there was his grandmother's tea set in his mom's walnut china cabinet in the front room. How does a dumb guy like him know whom to trust with priceless heirlooms and generations old keepsakes, the very ones his mother treasured and loved?

He raked a hand over his scalp, finally thinking what a fast sale and horse auction really meant to a guy who'd lived a transient life the last years. A guy who'd been on the move since the day he'd stormed past those magnificent live oaks and left home, never guessing it would be the last time he'd see them. Or his parents. Back then he'd been a young man filled with righteous rage and a big opinion of himself.

But now? Coming home had been heart breaking and eye-opening. *The Lost Chaparral* offered what he'd been looking for since he'd left. A place to land. A future. A home. And Jess.

He cast a sideways glance at the lady riding tall and happy in the saddle to his right, her silly looking foo-foo mutt trotting alongside, when it wasn't diving into gopher holes or chasing every blessed bird it spooked. Jess liked Tango, Smoke could tell. She kept stroking the mare's neck and ruffling her mane, leaning down to whisper sweet nothings. Tango was an easy mare to fall in love with.

The morning felt surreal, as if when he woke up and this new day would be just a dream. As if Jess would disappear back to New York. For the first time in months, the darkness when he'd fallen asleep last night hadn't stifled him in despair. He'd slept like a baby cuddled in her arms. He'd woken energized, and until Lassiter showed up, he'd felt like a man again. Not a has-been.

Scrubbing a hand over his face, Smoke banished his anger at Lassiter, and concentrated on Jess. Her skinny ass looked damned fine cradled in Tango's hand-tooled leather saddle. Better yet, Jess looked pretty damned fine lying in his arms this morning. Soft. Warm. Naked. He couldn't remember waking up when the world had felt as right as it did then.

Why she'd never owned her own horse still baffled him, but even as a kid, she'd borrow one from Montoya herd to compete in barrel-racing. Preferably a mare. Back then it was Rascal, an expensive registered quarter horse Smoke suspected his dad had bought just for the little neighbor girl who liked to race. Jess had an affinity for horses, and Smoke was just realizing that Caleb had had a way of smoothing the path for his son and his son's friends. That summer, Rascal spent more time with Jess than in her stall at the Montoya ranch.

The things a guy remembers...

Caleb Montoya. Insightful. Generous. Stern, but known to literally give the shirt off his back to a man down on his luck. Or to a little girl.

Ethan West. Dreamer. Party animal. The guy you wanted on your side after a rousing home game when the losing team came calling for a fight.

And always Jess. Smoke didn't have one good childhood memory without her in it.

"Oh, look! A bluebird!"

He didn't bother hunting for the flash of sapphire at the corner of his eye. He'd seen enough scrub jays in his life, but he'd never seen anything like Jess's enthusiasm for life before. Radiant. Happy. Damn, she looked good with her old cowboy hat pushed back on her ebony tangles, and the sun bright on her face. Did she ever stop smiling?

Life seemed to agree with her, and because it did, it agreed with him, too. The air was sweeter this morning. Or maybe it just seemed sweeter because they were brushing through a field of alfalfa. The sun seemed brighter. Clearer. Or maybe that was due to the storm-washed air and the optimistic weather report. Hell, even the prospect of three funerals didn't weigh on Smoke as much as he'd expected.

That reminder checked the good vibes of the day. He'd been so busy clearing the trees yesterday and loving Jess this morning, that he hadn't yet visited the funeral parlor or his parents' lawyer. Everything could still change.

But Lassiter's outrageous offer to Jess, as rude as it was, also made Smoke think. Made him wonder. Was selling *The Lost Chaparral* the right thing to do? Why wasn't it? Did he intend to stay in Texas? Or should he abandon his ties to America and keep on seeing the world like he had been. Somehow, that didn't seem so smart anymore. Or so necessary. A way had been cleared for his return home, by an F5 no less.

But then again, maybe this positive spin on life was just because of Jess. She'd always had a wild enthusiasm. He used to be like that. But the last couple of years had been more of an endurance test than an unquenchable thirst to see the world. Maybe it was time to come home. To stop running...

Jess kicked Tango up alongside him and Chip. "Whatcha thinking about, cowboy?" she asked, one brow arched salaciously and temptation glimmering in her eye.

Damned if a tender thing called a smile didn't tug at the hard, thin line of his stubborn lips. It had been doing that more and more since last night. "Not sex," Smoke muttered.

Surprising, but true. Sort of. He could always be persuaded.

"Oh, darn," she giggled, her head ducked into her shoulders like a little girl. "You're going to make me wait?"

Smoke liked the sound of that. This woman loved life, and she loved him. A guy couldn't get any luckier than to have Tess to come home to at the end of the day. Or to wake up with every morning.

"Follow me," he said as he reined Chip toward the creek that cut through the lower Montoya parcel. It wasn't long ago that he, Ethan, and Jess were three kids out of school for the summer and flying high on rope swings over the creek, carefree and ridiculously happy every day.

Caleb Montoya. Smoke had to admit his old man wasn't all bad. He'd done a lot for his family and neighbors over the years, and now Smoke was headed toward the shade of yet something else his old man had thoughtfully planted and left behind. More trees.

The ones the tornado took had been planted years and years ago by someone else, but the sycamores along the creek bank were fast growers that Caleb planted. They supplied shade and sturdy branches, just what every kid needed to climb up into and jump out of.

Smoke dropped off Chip's broad back before Jess had the chance to dismount. He snagged Tango's reins from her fingers and curved his hands to her waist, lifting her off the patient mare and into his arms. Setting Jess to her feet, he let the reins drop. The horses weren't going anywhere, not after a lazy ride in the sun, and not with a cool drink of water at their feet.

While Chip and Tango ambled for the creek, he headed for the nearest tree trunk, her hand still in his. He needed something to lean against while he held his lady. He didn't dare lay alongside the creek with her hot body. Not yet. There'd be no talking then.

"It's peaceful here," he murmured, toying with her hair, his back to a wide sycamore.

"Mmm," she purred, her hat hanging off her back and her arms once more around his neck. Her soft sweet breasts flush against his chest. Damn, she was a little thing. He stood a good foot taller and probably outweighed her by a hundred pounds. Yet she fit inside his body like a pearl inside an oyster.

"Remember the day we sloughed school? The day Ethan got his arm caught in the rope swing?" she asked.

"When he got the ugly burn that nearly took his arm off?" Yeah, Smoke remembered.

Just that fast, Ethan was there with them, yelling *'Cowabunga!'* and running pell-mell off the creek bank into the deep end of the creek. Doing belly flops. Imitating Disney's Goofy falling down a snowy mountain on skis with a long and loud, *'Ya-hoo-o-o-o-o-o!'* Pounding his chest like Tarzan before he dived off the homemade diving board nailed up high in the sturdy tree.

After he'd trimmed a few branches for a safer dive.

After he'd taken time out of his busy workday to tend to the demands of a few rowdy neighbor kids. And his son.

Caleb wasn't a monster. Just opinionated. Just bullheaded.

It was interesting the memories that popped in the clear light of day. The good times Smoke had forgotten. The family picnics with just him and his folks. But along with them came the ugly day Caleb had bellowed that Smoke was a flaming idiot to have voted like he had and then to choose to fight for Uncle Sam. He'd said that he'd always thought his son was smarter, but he guessed he was wrong. Of course then Caleb had mixed in his high-handed opinion about higher learning and going off to college. That if Smoke really were as smart as he thought he was, he'd buckle down and get to work running the ranch instead, that he'd leave his high and mighty ideas of saving America and freedom to men who had nothing to live for.

Caleb's last words: *'There's the door. Don't come back...'*

Smoke had always found it odd that an immigrant whose family had fought tooth and nail to come to America, could so easily forget how precious the land of freedom was. But in the end, it wasn't his father or mother's fault that he'd left *The Chaparral.* It was his. He'd let Caleb run him off. Well, no more.

Smoke flattened his palm between Jess's shoulder blades partly to feel her heat and her heartbeat, but mostly for the balance she'd always brought to his life. For the first time in a long while, he didn't feel the need to look over his shoulder and guard his back. He felt grounded. Oddly at peace. At home.

"This is my ranch now," he admitted out loud. "The house. The horses. This creek. Even that old rope swing and all the trees. Lassiter was right. Two hundred and eighteen acres, from the road to the slough south, is now mine." *Isn't that a kick in the head?*

"And I own a herd of cows," Jess chuckled. "Thirty-six altogether. Me. A high fashion model from New York City. I feel as if someone should be saying, *'Get the rope'* like in that salsa commercial."

"Longhorns," he corrected. "Why'd Ethan invest in them anyway?"

Jess looked north to where the herd grazed, placidly chewing their cud in the morning sunshine. "Ethan was the rancher, you know that. He wasn't born with the wanderlust you and I were.

Ever since our parents died, all he wanted was to be left alone. I was the drama queen—"

"You were a damned good barrel racer." Smoke wouldn't let her diminish herself. This woman was a natural in the saddle. She must never forget that. She should've been Sunnyvale's rodeo queen instead of Miss Texas. But the truth ran deeper than that. The day Jess lost her mom and dad, she'd lost part of her soul, too. Like him, she'd been looking in all the wrong places for her brand of peace. What if all they needed was what they'd left behind?

"And you were always mad," she said softly, her fingers on his chin as she turned in his arms.

Oh, that. Tugging her flat against his belly, he hooked his fingers in her belt loops and looked down into her pretty moss-green eyes. "It started in eighth grade when we studied the Vietnam conflict," he told her quietly. "The way America turned tail at the end. The way we lost the war. The way politics and Hollywood influenced the outcome. My dad saw everything in black and white. I didn't agree with him. He thought I should. You know how it goes."

This is my house, and as long as you live here...

Yeah, right. Smoke let the hateful words fade away. They didn't need to be voiced again.

Jess's fingertips stroked the thickening scruff on his cheeks that resembled a coarse beard more than whiskers. He'd needed a shave for days now. "Ethan and I could hear you and your dad fighting some nights," she told him.

"I can imagine. Mom said we were both stubborn and bullheaded. She said we were exactly alike, that's why we fought. We both had to be right."

"It's good to believe strongly in your convictions."

He leaned into her gentle touch. "It's good to come home, too. I've made up my mind. I've decided."

She straightened in his arms. But damn it, this had to be said out loud. Only then would he know if it was the right thing to do or another harebrained idea. He'd had a few of those.

Jess's brows arched. Her pretty eyes widened. Her fingers fluttered up to his neck in encouragement. "Yes?" she breathed, a funny haze shifting over her countenance.

"I'm not selling the place," he told her firmly. Absolutely. Unequivocally.

There. Finally. He was home and by hell, he meant to stay.

Chapter Thirteen

"Well, hell's bells," Jessie sputtered as she shut her big mouth before flies flew in and more stupidity flew out. Damn it. Why she had expected a marriage proposal wasn't the smartest thing in the world in the first place. After all, they'd only been together one night. He hadn't even said he loved her yet, but Smoke had gotten so serious all of a sudden. A proposal seemed possible. Her silly heart had lied to her, darn it, and told her it could happen.

Big surprise. It didn't. He hadn't even said he'd loved her, and there she was with tears suddenly blurring her eyes and—

Hell's bells, indeed.

Raising her clenched fist to her mouth, she coughed into it, just to clear her throat, mind you. It gave her a reason to duck out of his arms and turn away from that muscled chest that she had no business thinking she had a right to snuggle into. Not yet. It really was too soon. She had no hold on Smoke, and she should've been smarter. Men didn't sweep women off their feet any more. This was the twenty-first century.

"Goo-o-o-d," she breathed out like she meant it. "I'm staying, too."

Jess swallowed hard to get her brain out of fairytale land where happily-ever-after was a shoe-in for Cinderella. This was reality. Not a castle. And she wasn't Cinderella. What the hell had come over her?

"I don't think you should sell, either," Smoke muttered, his brows furrowed like he'd expected a different response, like he couldn't figure her out. "Especially not to Lassiter."

"Well, of course, you don't," she came back at him, embarrassed and off-balance from having her ridiculous feminine expectations dashed to the ground. "But what do I need with a ranch and cattle? I have a job in New York."

One dark brow arched, matching the arc to his lip. "I thought you weren't going back?"

"Yeah, well..." The roar of a motorcycle engine filtered through the trees, giving her an out. "Oh, look. Someone's at your house. You've got company."

Smoke glowered at her, his back against the tree and his muscular arms crossed over his chest. It looked like he'd just closed his heart behind those steel bands again. "Whoever they are, they can wait. Tell me right here and now, Jessie. Are you going back to New York City or not?"

She tugged her hat back on and leveled it low on her forehead, shading her eyes. "You know what? I don't want to think about that right now. Let's shelve this discussion for another day when we've got more time. You have company, I've got chickens to feed, and I need to discuss my contracts with a good lawyer before I make any firm decisions. Let's go."

Tango was an easy mare to catch. Jessie hopped back into the safety of the saddle, needing distance from the man who'd taken her to the stars last night, then dropped her flat on her dumb butt this morning. She knew he loved her, but damn. That man needed to spit it out before she gave any more of her tattered heart away. She still had a funeral to get through, and this morning's ride was a stupid idea. She should've fixed breakfast, so he had a full stomach to think on. Maybe things would've turned out differently.

Giving Tango a gentle kick in the ribs, she said, "Race you back."

Tango's hindquarters bunched before the mare launched into a full gallop. Smoke couldn't see her because he wasn't on horseback yet, and she had a good head start. He couldn't see her tears, either.

Damn it! Why'd I fall for that? Why'd I let myself think I was anything more than another easy lay for a tough guy, who probably has a girl in every port around the world? Isn't that what Navy SEALs do? Isn't that one of their macho calling cards? Their modus operandi? Bed 'em and love 'em and leave 'em? Tell 'em a lie to get what you want? Love the one you're with, or some other stupid male bullshit like that?

Gah! Her foolish heart hurt. She galloped Tango back to the stable, needing to feel the thunder under her butt instead of the lightning strike in her heart. Life didn't get any better than this. Jump into bed. Jump to conclusions. Maybe New York wasn't so bad after all. At least *there* she knew the rules. Screw everybody.

Jessie was at the hitching post before Smoke and Chip caught up with her. Dropping to her feet, she had Tango's stirrup flipped over the saddle horn before Smoke's boots hit the ground.

"Damn it, Jess," he growled. "What the hell was that all about? Why'd you run out on me?"

She shot him the barest glance, chin nodding at the biker standing at his front door to get him to stop looking at her. "Nothing. I've just got lots to do before the funeral. I still haven't taken a decent suit down to the parlor for Ethan. I've got" —for lack of enough air to breathe while she ranted— "I don't know, stuff to do."

"Jess. Look at me."

I don't want to! Go away!

Instead of meeting his eyes, she focused on loosening the girth and tugging the belly strap off Tango. "Go see who came to visit," she urged. "I'll take care of the horses. Don't worry. We'll get together later."

The man just wouldn't quit. Smoke latched onto the nape of her neck with one of those big manly hands and forced her head up and her eyeballs along with it. What could she do? She blinked hard and looked at him, damn it. Her lower lip started quivering, and those big old tears spilled over, and...

And now he smiles! She could've kicked his ass.

"Come here, Jess," he murmured, pulling her into his arms, melting the ice of her emotional outburst. Turning her knees to jelly. "Come here, baby." Like that sweet nickname helped. He used to call her baby as a tease, he'd just never said it so tenderly.

A sob wrenched up her throat. She let him pull her in under his chin, her ear over his heart again, and his hand tangled in her hair. Damn it, he hadn't touched her intimately, yet her body transformed into a feline—feminine and blatantly sensual. Needing to be stroked. Loving his touch.

He pressed a warm moist kiss to her forehead that really didn't help. She loved this moody man with his dark eyes and darker spirit. She'd loved him for years, but never thought she'd see him again, only now...

Jessie shifted her stubborn weight off one boot and settled easily into his arms. "Smoke," she said simply. What else was there to say?

"You're hungry and tired," he muttered, his tone deep and rumbling in her ear. "I think we need to get you back into bed. Soon."

That almost sounded promising. She swallowed her pride. "It's just that—"

"Hey! Smoke! You gonna be all day?"

A woman? Jessie's eye widened. She tipped her face to that annoying troll standing in a full set of leathers at Smoke's front door, with *her* hands on *her* hips and a raft of white blonde hair streaming in the breeze behind *her*. *Who the hell is she?*

"Colby?" Smoke called out, his palm lifted to his forehead shading his eyes. "Is that you? Stay there, I'll be right up." But to Jessie he said, "Are you sure you'll be okay?"

Jessie looked up at that strong, tanned neck to the light in his eyes. He knew Colby Whoever-She-Was, damn him. Worse, he sounded happy to see her. That shouldn't have bothered Jessie, but it did. The green-eyed monster lifted its spiked head and rattled its scales, her last nerve along with it. She'd seen enough.

"Yes," she lied, untangling from his arms. "Go talk to your friend. I'll be fine."

Just fine.

Chapter Fourteen

Smoke ambled over the field to Colby. Damn, she was a sight for sore eyes.

"What are you doing here?" he asked the gal who'd moved into the apartment next to his place in Cambodia a year ago. Her bathroom pipes sprang a leak the same day, so she'd ended up on his couch a few nights. Nothing serious.

The plumber came a week later. The pipes got fixed, but by then, Smoke had gotten used to having someone around. The minute she told him to 'move it' on her way to the bathroom, that she wouldn't hurt him, she was in like Flint.

Colby was a straight shooter and an easy friend to talk to. She never pried and she didn't push. It took her all of two minutes to give up her lease, but not her freedom, and she'd moved in with Smoke. They'd been roommates since. Shared the rent and an occasional bottle. A few laughs. A few nightmares. Nothing more.

"Why the hell didn't you tell me both your parents died in that storm?" She stabbed a pointed fingernail into his chest, her chin lifted like she meant to knock him over if he didn't speak up. "Huh? You take off for home, and you can't be square with me? Jesus!"

Smoke shrugged, not needing to defend himself against this tough gal. "It's good to see you, too."

She slapped his face with one of those half-hearted slaps she dished out to guys she half-liked. Heaven help the man she really liked. "Back atcha. You got some place I can drop for a few hours? I've been flying all night. I'm wasted."

Smoke waved a hand toward his parents', ahem, *his* hacienda, and damned if his father's voice didn't speak up with, "Mi casa es su casa." Warmth crept up his neck. Holy hell. It didn't get any weirder than that.

Colby cocked her head at him. "Have you been drinking? You look happy, or something. What's wrong with you?"

Where to begin? He decided to start with the woman who'd changed his life, but where was she? "Jess?" he called out, but the horses were out of sight. She must've taken them inside the stable to brush them down.

Colby snaked her arm through his. "You can tell me all about it, while I show you my new ride."

He'd already noticed. "When did you decide you like Harleys?"

"Not just any Harley," she purred, the sun light in her eyes pure gold. "It's a Dyna Low Rider. Previously owned. I picked it up for a song and a prayer outside Dallas. Take it for a spin. You'll like it."

"But can you lift it once you forget to engage the kickstand and it drops like a ton of bricks?"

She chuckled, shaking her head and sending those golden locks flying. "I know, huh? Trust me, it's heavy, too. Just my luck I'd drop it when no one's around to help me get it on its wheels again. The guy at the Harley store showed me how to do it, but I might need to practice a bit before I head out."

"You're not going back to Cambodia?"

She blew out a long sigh. "Not sure yet. I've got family in Boston, my mom. She hasn't been well. I'll figure it out once I'm back on the road. If all else fails, yeah. I might have to sell my bike, but Cambodia's good enough."

Wasn't that the truth?

Colby Quaid. Rough and tumble former Army sergeant. One of the first female Rangers. As daring as they came. Prone to come up swinging if you were stupid enough to startle her from a deep sleep. Independent as hell. A woman of uncommon valor. How they'd ever ended up rooming together in far off Cambodia only testified to their demons. She had hers. He had his.

"So why are you really here?"

"No reason." She slouched out of her leather jacket, revealing a tiny pink T-shirt with the HOG eagle emblem over her magnificent chest. It looked damned good with the three-dimensional effect. "I just figured it was time to move on. The place got quiet once you left."

He wasn't buying that. "I've only been gone a couple days."

"Yeah, well..." She stared off into space. "You know how it is. I hate to stay in one place too long."

That he understood. "How'd you find out my folks died?"

"I figured it had to be serious, the way you sounded the morning you called, so I Googled Sunnyvale. I saw your parents' obits," she admitted. "I'm sure sorry, Smoke. I know things were hard between you and your folks, but they were still your folks. Them passing at the same time has to be tough. When's the funeral?"

"Tomorrow. You staying?"

Again with the far-off stare. "Not sure. You know how I hate those things. I might since it's you though."

He tugged her against him. "Come on, girlfriend. I've got someone I want you to meet."

Colby smacked his chest. "Gah, what is that smell? A new men's cologne I'll never buy?"

Smoke took a deep breath of the great Texas outdoors mingled with a hint of Chip; surprised it smelled as sweet on him as it did. "It's pure horseshit, girlfriend. This is my land and my horses. Wait 'til you see them."

"Your horses?" she asked, her brows arced in surprise. "Are you planning on staying here? Seriously?"

The idea didn't seem so crazy now that she'd said it. "Yeah. I'm done running. The neighbor lady and I go way back. Jessie West. You'll like her."

"No way." Cassidy stopped walking long enough to cuff his shoulder. "Are you shittin' me? Jessie West? As in the famous model, Jessie West? You know her?"

There it was again, that thing tugging his lips. Smiling almost hurt—in a really good way. He was so damned proud of Jess. "She's the one but keep it on the down low. Her brother died in a freak accident after the storm. She'd like to keep out of sight."

Colby ran two pinched fingers across her lips like she was closing a zipper. "You won't hear it from me," she mumbled, then forgot all about the zipped lip "But are you telling me there's something between you and this chick from New York?" She punched him a good one then, clipping his shoulder. "Damn you, Smoke. How long's this been going on?"

Ouch. He loved this feisty, crazy woman. Platonically, but yeah, he loved Colby. She was all spitfire, big attitude, and smart mouth. She never cut him any slack, but she hadn't stopped caring about him, either. She was like Colby. They looked out for each other. Had each other's backs. End of story.

"Don't jump the gun," he groused to throw her off track. "Jess and I just hooked up last night and—"

A big grin split Colby's face. She clenched her fists and did the hip thrust thing a few times. "You mean you hooked up as in... hubba, hubba hooked up?"

"Knock it off," he muttered, palming the stable door open, hoping Jess hadn't heard Colby's taunt, but damn. Some jerk had taped another real estate flyer on the stable door with, *You'll be sorry!* highlighted in bright neon yellow. "This is getting old."

"Whatcha got there?" Colby peered around his arm. "You're selling?"

"No." Lassiter' high-pressure tactics were unbelievable. "Never mind. Come say hello to Jess and be nice. Jess!" he called out calmly to not spook the horses.

But she and Fluffy weren't there, only Chip, Tango and the mares.

What the hell?

Chapter Fifteen

"Now, you listen here, you ungrateful shrew. You *will* be on that runway in Cannes by Sunday, and you *will* jerk that thong up your tight little ass, or I'll sue you for breach of contract. Believe it. I'll take every last penny you've got. You owe me, West. You're not getting away with this!"

"No, Fernando, you listen," Jessie snapped back at her once kindly agent, now turned into Attila the Hun. She'd contacted a good lawyer in New York, who'd already advised Sonoma that Jessie West was no longer his client, nor would she attend the event in Cannes. Her phone hadn't stopped ringing since.

"This is your last warning, Freddy," she declared.

He wouldn't like that. The press tagged Sonoma a *Freddie Kruger-type* stalker after a nasty rumor surfaced about him and a glamorous Brazilian model. She'd never filed charges, but he'd challenged every rag that dared print the libelous taunt. "Contact my lawyer. You have his number. Goodbye."

"Don't call me Freddy, you bitch!"

Cringing at her audacity, Jessie disconnected despite his very loud objection. *Maybe I shouldn't have fired that last volley.*

But she had. Resolutely, she turned her cell phone off, unplugged her landline before another call came in, and popped a K-cup in Ethan's coffee maker. A good shot of caffeine would get her through the rest of the day.

As if things couldn't get any worse, she'd come home to another flyer from the man with two last names. Jenkins Lassiter. The jerk. Then the nice lady at the funeral parlor had left another terse voice mail begging her to *please* bring Ethan's best suit so the poor man could be dressed for his own funeral.

Out of sheer nerves, she'd fried up the two pounds of thick-cut, peppered bacon she'd found in Ethan's refrigerator, thinking Smoke would come looking for her. He hadn't. He was still over at his ranch with his lady friend. To top it off, with all her phone calls, Jessie burned the bacon, and the house smelled like the wrong kind of smoke.

Damn it. Nothing had gone right.

After one last hopeful glance to the Montoya hacienda but no sight of Smoke, she buckled down to business. Smoke was obviously too busy and poor Ethan needed something decent to be buried in. She'd finally decided on which western shirt she liked best, then his newest pair of Levi's. Grabbing those out of his closet, she selected the least scuffed boots she could find, his fiddler-brown, square-toed, Ariat shitkickers.

And reality struck. Her legs gave out. Jessie sank to the floor beside his unmade bed, tears caught in her throat. From the rich grain of the leather to the sturdy heel, to the lack of fancy stitching on his leather boots. The silver snaps in lieu of buttons on his shirt. The texture of ordinary cotton beneath her trembling fingers. Not silk. Certainly not fancy. These things were Ethan, through and through. A simple man. Rough stock. Leather. Not exotic alligator or snakeskin. Part workhorse. Part party animal. One hundred percent her buddy and her dearest, sweetest friend.

And gone…

Jessie lifted his shirt to her nose and ended up burying her face in all she had left of her brother. A teary sob jerked out of her. "I miss you," she told him from the saddest part of her heart. "How can I go on without you, huh? Did you ever think of that before you started hacking on that stupid tree? Did you ever think of me?"

Did you ever think of him?

And there it was, her just reward served up with a cherry on top for all those shallow pageants and contests and foolish, foolish dreams. This sad day was only the echo of what she'd set in motion years ago. On the day she'd left Ethan and Smoke standing in the rodeo arena. The day she'd left the best parts of herself behind.

Jessie gathered the pieces of her broken heart and every last one of her poor choices, and she stood. The past was done, but every day forward, every step and every decision she made from now on, would be due to Ethan and the faith he'd put in her. He'd believed she could fly, well fly she would. Again. Someday.

If anyone could pull this change in career and heart and soul off, Jessie West sure as hell could. If only because Ethan had always and forever believed in his little sister. Plugging in her house phone, she made one quick call.

Mr. Stauffer arrived ten minutes later. "You're looking better today," he said, his kindly brown eyes keeping track of her in his rearview mirror.

"That's because you can see who I am this time, huh?"

He offered a gracious wink. "It's okay, Miss Jessie. I knew it was you last night, too. This is a tough time you're going through. Folks will understand."

She swallowed hard past the dry knot in her throat. "Will they? Will they understand why I'm the biggest bitch on the East Coast, too?"

He shrugged, his wise, older gaze reflecting no judgment or surprise. "Looking beautiful every single day would be enough to make me crabby right along with you."

"That's not why," she murmured, her gaze on the rows of knee-high corn flying by. How could she admit to herself, much less everyone else, that she'd made the wrong decision by leaving her hometown years ago? How did she get people to understand that fame and fortune haven't made her happy? That they never would? That the harder she'd worked, the more she'd seemed to slip-and-slide into more risqué situations than she felt comfortable with? That she felt as if she'd prostituted her body to sell diamonds and cars, swimming suits and cosmetics? That until she'd come home to Texas, she'd been afraid she was losing her soul—or had already lost it?

Jessie, gulped past the hollow feeling in the center of her chest where her scruples used to be. The only time she'd felt like herself had been with Smoke last night and early this morning. Even that special feeling now seemed somehow diminished. Who knew his girlfriend would track him down? Hell, who knew he had one?

"What's your name?" she asked quietly.

Mr. Stauffer shot her a genuine smile in the mirror. "Lincoln Jefferson Stauffer, ma'am. My mama named me Lincoln after the best president this country ever had, Jefferson after her daddy."

"Lincoln Jefferson, hmm." She let it roll off her tongue with a deep sigh. "It fits you. So what's your sad story? Are you married? Any children?"

He bobbed his head, his hair now grizzled and white with age. "Yes, ma'am. One wife. Six kids.

Seventeen grandchildren and one great grandson. Life's been good to me. Not sure I have a sad story, though. For the most part, I've been blessed."

"Have you ever made a mistake that was too big to fix?" she asked softly. "I mean, I thought I fixed it, only I think I just made it worse, and now..." She blinked, her emotions climbing up her throat, where they could get her into serious trouble.

Lincoln Jefferson Stauffer pulled his van to the curb in front of the funeral parlor and swung his arm over the seat. "There isn't any such thing as a mistake too big to fix, Miss West. There are just big lessons and little lessons in life. It's what you learn from them what's important. Life's too short to be scared of the future. What's troubling you, honey?"

Her eyes misted over while her sad story poured out. "I don't want to be a super model anymore, Lincoln Jefferson. I don't want to be rich, and I don't want to be popular. I just want to be me again, and I want Smoke to love me, and hold me, and kiss me, and..." *Wah, wah, wah!* If that meltdown didn't make her sound like a spoiled two-year old, nothing did.

All at once Mr. Stauffer was sitting next to her in the back seat with one leg out the door, one arm wrapped around her shoulder and patting her arm like he could fix everything. "There, there, now don't you fret. Things are gonna be okay."

It had to be her hormones. "No, they won't," she squeaked. "Nobody likes me, and they call me bitch behind my back, and you know what? They're right, but I'm only a bitch because I'm not happy anymore, and I'm tired of being pushed to do things I don't want to do, and I'm tired of living alone with just Fluffy for company, and now Smoke's got a girlfriend, and..." She sucked in a deep, shuddering breath after that long run-on. "It's not me."

Wah! Wah! Wah!

She leaned into Mr. Stauffer's shoulder, for the first time noticing he wore something that no one in New York would be caught dead in unless they were transients and lived on the street. A homemade, hunter green knitted sweater. She took a deep breath of what had to be Old Spice, and she calmed herself. Jessie pinched the fuzzy yarn on his sleeve cuff, rubbing her fingers back and forth on the old-fashioned weave of purl one, knit two. "Did your wife make this for you?" she asked, her voice weak and raspy.

"She did," he said proudly. "Georgia's been taking care of me fifty-five years, now."

"That's a long time." Jessie swiped her runny nose once before Lincoln dragged a packet of tissues up from his pocket and offered her one. "She must love you a lot."

He nodded, rocking her there in his cab in the gentle Texas spring sunshine until she composed herself and said, "Thanks, and I'm sorry. I don't usually fall apart like this." The tears started again, but she was prepared. She had Kleenex. "Guess I'd better go in and see my brother."

God, this day just plain sucked.

Mr. Stauffer helped her up out of the vehicle like the gentleman he was, then locked his cab and accompanied her into the parlor. "Don't you worry 'bout a thing, Miss West. You called me, and I'm here for you. I'll keep you from falling apart. This is what friends do."

CHAPTER SIXTEEN

"Hey, umm, Smoke," Colby muttered at the front door. "You might want to come see this. Looks like your girlfriend's place is on fire."

He scrambled to the front porch to see puffs of black smoke lifting high over Jess's house. "Shit, yeah. I'll be right back."

"I'm coming with you."

It didn't take long to jog the path between the houses. Running up the back steps two at a time, he tried the knob. Locked. "Jess!" he bellowed, pounding at the window, hoping to see her inside. Only Fluffy came to the glass, his tongue lolling and his eyes bright like he wanted to play.

"Hey, get your ass over here. It's not the house that's burning," Colby called to him from the east side. "It's the chickens!"

He jumped the porch railing. Sure enough, the coop was ablaze and a couple chickens, too. The rest of the frightened birds were panicked, trying to escape the conflagration crackling at their rear. Clucking and bawking, they'd piled on each other in a corner of the wire, a couple of hens running back and forth shrieking, their feathers smoking. The coop wasn't more than sixteen feet square, but it was a complete loss, it's shingled roof melting and dripping tar into the flaming floorboards.

Colby grabbed a coiled garden hose at the foundation of the house and turned on the water, while Smoke jerked the makeshift gate off its hinges. When she laid down a healthy spray, he was rewarded with a face full of panicked spurs and wet feathers.

Smoke ducked in through the low and narrow gate. The rest of the chickens could be rounded up later, but he wouldn't allow the injured ones to suffer. Catching them was a challenge, and he slid more than once on waterlogged chicken shit. But finally, he caught the two injured birds and quickly twisted their necks to put them out of their misery.

Tossing them out of the pen to the lawn, he turned back on what was left.

Flames sprouted up from the inside nesting boxes, but the question of the day remained. How the hell did a chicken coop in the shade burst into flames, when the ground around it was still soaked from the storm that had spawned an F5 a few days earlier?

"That's enough water," he advised Colby while he investigated. Interesting. The front of the coop wasn't burned as badly as the rear. He checked for an electrical cord running from the house, thinking maybe Ethan kept an incubator inside the coop. No incubator. No brooder, either. Just the sneaky suspicion that this was arson.

Jenkins Lassiter's threatening flyer came to mind. Was this what his *You'll be sorry* meant? Was this his way of frightening Jess into selling? Dumbass sure didn't know Jess if it was.

"Where's your girlfriend?" Colby asked, her nose wrinkled at the unpleasant stench of wet chicken feathers and soot.

"She doesn't have a car," Smoke replied evenly, "but she might've called a cab. She said she had to take some clothes into the funeral parlor for Ethan."

"Who's Ethan?" Colby asked quietly, the hose once again coiled tight against the foundation of the house.

"Her brother." Smoke's gut clenched. "My friend. He was clearing a fallen tree after the storm, and it rolled on him. Killed him."

His gaze shifted to the pile of sawdust in the lawn where once a giant tree had stood. Ethan should've known better, damn it. Between all that had happened yesterday, Smoke hadn't yet paid his friend due respect. Acid bloomed in his gut. It was true. Ethan was gone. *God. Damn.*

"Maybe you ought to go find her," Colby suggested. "Mortuaries are no place to be alone when you're feeling like crap."

Smoke nodded. He needed to visit Ethan, too. "Good idea. I'll leave once I've got the chickens rounded up."

It didn't take long to shoo the nervous birds inside the West's barn and shut them in. Smoke didn't care if they all roosted on Ethan's John Deere tractor. At least they were accounted for, miserable, but alive.

"Go on," Colby urged when the task was done. "Jessie needs you. Go get her."

"I should shower first."

She slanted one of her truly evil eyes in his direction. "Oh, for hell's sake, no woman in her right mind cares what you smell like on a miserable day like this, Smoke. She's going to be damned happy you cared enough to show up. I would, so move it. Get the hell out of here."

He nodded, the muscles in his calves twitching to run to Jess, to wrap her up tight and safe again. "There are sandwiches in the fridge and cupcakes on the counter. Help yourself."

Colby eyed the two dead birds in the grass. "Uh-uh. I'm thinking grilled chicken. Hurry back. I'll save you some."

CHAPTER SEVENTEEN

"Hi," Jessie said quietly.

Not like Ethan answered.

The mortician had done a good job. Ethan looked like he was sleeping. He'd been temporarily dressed in a plain white button-down shirt, but his tanned skin looked natural. His cheeks were just the right shade of healthy pink. His brows weren't furrowed like they usually were, just calm and peaceful. His big hands were folded serenely on his chest, his mangled legs hidden beneath the shroud. One finger had a flesh-colored bandage on it, but that was Ethan for you. His lips looked chapped, probably because he'd licked them when he was hard at work. When he was concentrating. Like he would've been doing while he used the chainsaw on that tree.

Still...

She fell apart now that she was face to face with the brother she'd deserted. Utter grief crawled up her throat to choke her.

Lincoln stood faithfully at her side, massaging a gentle circle on her shoulder blade. "He was always proud of you, Miss Jessie. We all knew who Ethan's famous sister was. He made sure of that."

Knowing she'd been careless with her only brother's love and affection, while he'd bragged her up, cut her to the quick. Her poor heart swelled to bursting with remorse and guilt.

"He was gonna marry Miss Crockett. Did you know?"

Jessie shook her head, wiping her eyes. "Dakota? No, I didn't," breathed out of her on a raspy sigh. She would've known if she'd ever called. If she'd cared.

Her broken heart cracked all over again.

"Don't you fret none, Miss Jessie. We've all been where you're at right now. Life gets busy, when you're young and burning the candle at both ends, doesn't it?" Lincoln asked. "I looked at my kids, when they were little, and the next time I turned around, they were graduating from college and having babies of their own. Yes, sir. Days go by quick as lightning bugs in June when we're young."

Jessie swallowed hard. "He... Ethan... He liked lightning bugs. We used to run through the fields on summer nights and see who could catch the most. Mom let us keep them in Mason jars with holes in the lids, but we had to let them go before we went to bed. He always made sure I caught more than he did. He was always looking out for me."

Lincoln made a soft grunt. "Sounds like Ethan was the perfect big brother."

She blinked hard, her eyes overflowing. "Yes, sir. He was." The sob sneaked up on her. "And I let him down."

Lincoln pulled her into his side. "No, you didn't. You owed it to yourself to figure out if that dream of yours was worth living. That's all you did. Now stop blaming yourself for taking a chance on spreading your wings. He wouldn't want that, would he?"

This day had turned into a rollercoaster ride of despair intermingled with momentary glimpses of hope and fortitude. She needed something more solid to hang onto. "I... I don't know anymore."

"Well, I do. What do you think Ethan would be saying if he were here today? Tell me."

She honestly didn't know, but he'd be grinning. Ethan was like that, happy from the inside out. He'd be proud, high-fiving everyone in sight and bragging her up like he used to do in their rodeo days. Then he'd pull her braids and boss her around.

Lincoln cleared his throat. "Caroline and Caleb are in the next room. If you don't mind, I'm going to visit them while you talk to your brother. Don't leave without me, you hear?"

Jessie nodded, her chest filled with regret for being the negligent little sister, when she could have been so much more. "I'm sorry. I should've been here, Ethan. I should've come home sooner and more often. I'm so sorry for being selfish and thoughtless and..." A sob hiccupped out of her. "I miss you. Nothing's going to be the same."

She bent her face to her brother's, tears dripping onto his cheek. "I wish I could do everything over again. I do. I wish I'd never left Sunnyvale. I could've been out there helping you with that tree. I could've... I should've..."

A gentle hand landed in the middle of her back. Jessie shook her head, not wanting to see who'd witnessed her breakdown.

"He loved you so much," a woman said quietly behind her.

Now she had to look. Jessie sucked back her tears. "Dakota?"

Dakota Crockett blinked hard, a tissue held to her puffy, red nose. "Yes. I'm here."

Jessie fell into her arms. "I'm so sorry," she whispered. "Maybe if I'd been—"

"Oh, hush. Ethan wouldn't have paid any more attention to you than he did me. You can't blame yourself for what happened, Jessie. That brother of yours was as hardheaded as you, but twice as stubborn. You know that. I told him to let the guys from the feed store help him take that tree apart, but would he listen? Heck, you know the answer to that. And here we are."

Jessie nodded, her face still dripping with tears. Talking with Ethan's girlfriend helped.

Dakota handed her another tissue. Then another. "If you're anything like me, you're going to need plenty of these. I've been going through them by the box full."

"I didn't know you were engaged," Jessie admitted.

"Hmmpf. Neither did I." Dakota swiped her swollen eyes with an already soggy tissue. "That crazy brother of yours never got around to asking, and now I find out he had big plans for us. That would've been nice to know before he up and got himself killed, don't you think? Damn him for putting that off. I could have a ring around this finger." She waggled her left hand. "I should smack him, while he's lying there pretending to be asleep, for all the trouble he's put us both through." Her voice rapped up higher as she finished, her tissue to her nose and tears streaming over her cheeks. "Darn him, Jessie. I loved him, and now he's gone."

It was Jessie's turn at compassion. She wrapped her arm around the woman who would've been her sister-in-law. "He procrastinated a lot, didn't he?" *Didn't we all?*

Dakota's brows furrowed like Scrooge's in Dickens Christmas story. "You think? That brother of yours could make Father Nickels down at Saint Leo's church swear. If he was ever on time, I didn't know it. If I wanted to see the previews, I'd have to tell him the movie started an hour earlier than it did, just to get him there in time. And don't you dare go blaming yourself for not keeping in touch. It's a two-way street. Did he ever call you? Did he ever write one single letter? I doubt it."

Dakota wore no makeup. Just sadness. Just like Jessie, she was a woman facing the cold hard truth. "Ethan was never good at writing or calling. You know that."

"But did he ever once visit you in New York? Did he see your apartment? I'll bet it's as glamorous as all get out."

Clenching her lips, Jessie shook her head. There was no way she could forgive herself. "He was going to visit, though."

Dakota's head bobbed, her short blonde hair too. "Yeah, right. He said all the right things, but we both know better. Ethan just kind of expected you'd do the calling and visiting, didn't he? That it was your job to keep in touch. Yes, that was my Ethan, lots of talk, not enough action." She leaned over the edge of the casket and traced her index finger over his lower lip. "But I loved him," she said softly, a catch in her voice, "and you're right. I'm going to miss him, too."

Jessie blew her nose, her heart breaking for all she and Dakota had lost, for what they'd have to live without. Ethan's lift-you-off-your-feet bear hugs. The hearty laughs that came from his belly. Beer parties and tailgating. College football on Saturday afternoons in the fall. Rodeo in the summer. If anything, he'd known how to live, and he went after what he'd wanted. The longhorns. Taking care of his baby sister when their parents died. Manning up. That damned tree. And eventually, when he got around to it... Dakota.

"Would you like to grab a cup of coffee?" she asked. "I'd love to know you better, Jessie. All I know is that you're some fancy model from New York City, but you seem more like a regular person now that I've met you. What do you say? The Rusty Nail makes a mean grilled chicken salad, and their prickly pear margaritas are to die for."

A sweet and salty drink actually sounded like a good idea.

Jessie's eyes filled when she turned to her brother. "This isn't goodbye," she told Ethan in no uncertain terms, her heart in her throat making every breath and every word a struggle. She blinked through the tears on her eyelashes. "Get dressed, Ethan. Be good while I'm gone and try to stay out of trouble." She leaned into his new resting place and placed a tender kiss on his forehead. "I'll always love you, big brother. Say hi to Mom and Dad for me."

Dakota didn't give her more time to cry. She twined her arm around Jessie's and declared, "There now. Let's go have a drink to honor Ethan's life. He might not have asked me, but I don't care. You're my sister now, and I have a feeling we're going to be best friends."

Jessie looked up and straight into the kindly face of Lincoln Jefferson Stauffer. "I see you found another ride home, young lady."

She held out her hand to him. "Come with us?"

He offered the crook of his elbow, and with a smile, he did.

Smoke missed Jess at Purdy's Funeral Home, but she'd been there. He could tell. Ethan looked good in his blue-checkered western shirt, his brown hair combed, all dapper and ready to—go.

He stared down at the tall, lean man lying in the casket. "Couldn't wait to use that fancy chainsaw, huh? You big dummy."

They'd been best buddies ever since Smoke could remember. Ethan was his age. His brown eyes were closed in peaceful repose, his hair combed for once in his rowdy life. The guy looked like he was sleeping, and Smoke didn't know what to say. It had been a long time and letters had been few and far between.

Memories of happier days flooded his head. Rodeos. Football games. Guy-talk about girls and parents. Ethan had always gotten along with his old man, yet it was the Montoya ranch that drew him and Jess, instead of the West ranch that drew Smoke. Maybe it was the horses. Ethan's parents weren't horse ranchers by nature. Back then they'd owned a dairy herd. They were farmers. Like Ethan.

What a waste.

"I love your sister," Smoke told his friend. "I'm going to marry Jess."

The clock out in the lobby chimed a gentle swell of *How Great Thou Art,* an odd comment on the day. It was time to go. Smoke reached into the casket and laid a gentle fist bump to Ethan's muscular shoulder. Leaning into his friend's ear, he let the words roll off his tongue, the same words he'd said too many times before. "Save a place at the table for me, brother. I'll see you later."

Next Smoke checked for Jess in his parent's room, but she wasn't there, either. Then he couldn't leave. He'd put this moment off, so in a roundabout way, it was a good thing the day's events forced his hand. His mother and father lay silently waiting. Caleb and Caroline.

Going to his mother first, Smoke looked down at her sweet, still, delicate face. "Hi, Mama," he whispered, his heart up high in his throat.

She looked so alive. Dark-haired and brown-eyed like him, she'd been born the second daughter of the wealthy De La Cruz family from Austin, Texas. At seventeen, his headstrong mother had married a dashing migrant worker from South America, a brash young man with high ambitions and little money. But Caleb Montoya wasn't just a hard worker. He was smart. After he became an American citizen, he made good on his promise to care for Caroline.

When he'd decided to dig her a duck pond, but struck oil, it was a sweet stroke of pure dumb luck. It was also an odd thing, just like the capricious path of the F5, since oil wasn't found on any neighboring ranches. God knew Clem Hardy had spent his last dime, drilling hole after hole, hoping to strike it rich like Caleb had. The Montoya streak of good luck was a continual source of discord with Clem.

Caroline looked at peace, her thick dark lashes curled like crescents over lightly blushed cheeks. Her lips had been touched up with just a trace of color, slightly bowed with her usual smile. Her brand of perfume wafted up from the open casket, tugging Smoke through memories of the last time she'd hugged him. Stories she'd read to him as a little boy snuggled into her warm, motherly body. Bed times. Bath times. She'd always smelled powdery and feminine. Sweet. Delicate, but strong.

He knelt, his forehead pressed to the side of her casket, his fingers gripping the edge, and his eyes closed. Smoke knew how to pray. He just hadn't done it in a while. The old words came easily. *Hail Mary full of grace... Our Father who art in heaven... Glory be to the Father and the Son... Remember, oh, most gracious Virgin Mary... Oh, my God, I am heartily sorry...*

And others.

He said all the prayers he knew because that would make his mother happy. Caroline could now rest in peace, knowing he still believed at some level. That he was still her son, the little boy she'd taught to pray. That he'd remembered.

She'd once explained why she'd named him Smoke, not your usual name for a firstborn child. But the day he was born, the oil well had caught fire. The blackest smoke billowed forth from Mother Earth for as long as Caroline's difficult labor lasted.

By the time Caleb and his crew extinguished the flames, Caroline's doctor delivered her firstborn, and Caroline took that as a sign from God. If smoke was good enough for Mother Earth, it was good enough for Caroline. She'd kissed the still wet baby boy in her arms and offered him back to God with, *In the name of the Father, and the Son, and the holy... Smoke.*

A smile breached his lips thinking about how serious she'd told this outlandish story many times over. Caroline loved her superstitious twists on her much-loved conventional religion. She said that was what gave piety its zest, its fire, and its soul.

So he grew up as Smoke, an oddly appropriate name given his eventual career path. Most SEAL brothers thought the name was a handle he'd been tagged with, like Reaper and Hawk, Digger and Bull. That it derived from his number of kills and his stone-cold rep. Maybe from the talent that he had for getting into tight places without being seen. For getting the toughest jobs done and getting out alive.

But no. His given name really was... Smoke. He'd just let people believe what they wanted to believe. Then scuttlebutt had created an aura to his reputation as a sniper, a mystique to the common, ordinary guy he really was. When the insurgents' bounty on his head climbed to a million American dollars, he just kept on keeping his head down and serving his country.

Caroline Montoya had never let him forget he was a gift from God, which made her seeming lack of love and affection these past years all the harder to accept or understand. She wasn't a timid little mouse of a wife. She'd stood up to Caleb often in the past, so why not when he'd exiled her only child from the loving embrace of *The Lost Chaparral?*

Another mystery Smoke might never unravel. He smoothed the back of his index finger over her cheek, not understanding why she hadn't sought shelter from that vicious storm. For a woman caught in the throes of an F5, so classified because of its winds in excess of two hundred and sixty miles per hour, her skin was remarkably clear of bruises and abrasions. Her nose wasn't broken, and there wasn't a visible hint of violence been inflicted on her that he could see.

He'd spoken with the funeral director, expecting closed caskets instead of open, but the man assured Smoke there were no broken bones on either of his parent's bodies, and no reason not to proceed with a proper viewing.

Maybe *The Lost Chaparral* was just that. Lost chances. Lost families. Lost mysteries.

Easing to his feet, Smoke dug deep in his pocket. He pulled up the lucky charm he'd carried with him every day in the Navy, her crystal rosary beads with its ornate silver crucifix. It was the design of this very cross he'd had tattooed on his left bicep in honor of her. The De La Cruz. *Of the cross.* Outcast or not, a son never forgot his mother.

"I'm not going back to Cambodia," he told her, "and I'm going to ask Jess to marry me. You always liked her. Thought you ought to know."

Carefully and tenderly, Smoke arranged the beads in Caroline's clasped fingers like she was praying, the crucifix upright and tucked between the index finger of her right hand and the thumb of her left. Caleb would've made some deprecating remark if he'd been there, but he wasn't, and that was good. This was mother and son time. Sacred time. The last time.

"There, now you're ready to go," Smoke whispered to the woman he would always love. His eyes brimmed as he leaned over the edge of her casket. "Goodbye," he breathed as he touched his warm lips to her cold skin. "I'll love you forever, Mama. Sleep tight. Pray for me, please?"

He'd no more than straightened and released a tremendous sigh when peace floated over him like a veil of calm from the other side. It was a lovely thought when a guy had to leave the first woman he'd ever loved behind.

Now for Caleb Montoya.

A son should feel more than disdain when eventually, he stands over the man who raised him, but there was no tenderness in Smoke's heart. No *'hi, Papa.'* No *'love you.'* Only regret for the way things had ended between them, for words he couldn't and wouldn't take back. Only sadness for the in-your-face *'Not in my house!'* his father never should've bellowed at his only son. For the anger. The silence.

He stared at the man, their battles over and the war lost for both of them. Caleb's thick black mustache had been neatly trimmed and combed. His chin was shaved. The worry grooves on his forehead didn't seem nearly as deep as Smoke remembered. His lips were still thin and stern, demanding, not bowed in gentle acceptance like Caroline's. His face was no more bruised or disfigured than his wife's. Still proud. Still arrogant. Still the same stern patriarch. It showed in the tilt of his chin, even in death.

His father's spicy aftershave drifted up from the casket, but the scent had always brought tension and unfulfilled expectation, while his mother's perfume brought comfort. Such opposites.

If Smoke had learned one thing as a child, it was that a father's love was conditional. Even that bolo tie with the Texas star around Caleb's neck, the one Smoke had made him for Father's Day when he was eight, was a joke. Caleb hadn't worn it when he'd been alive, not once that Smoke could recall.

Yes, he'd planted trees and he'd built tree houses and he'd put up rope swings for his son, but he'd also demanded payment in strict obedience at the snap of his fingers. There were no father son bedtime stories in Smoke's past. No tender goodnights. No gentle lessons learned other than, *'Do what you're told.'*

A badass SEAL shouldn't miss those things after all he'd seen and done, but Smoke did. Especially now. Especially here...

He looks just like you. His mother's words. Not his. But she was right. Smoke could see the resemblance. Damn. Same black brows. Same perpetual frown. What was there to say? They were too much alike to ever have gotten along, but now, there'd be no second chance to agree to disagree. No happy ending, either.

He drew in a deep breath and let it fill the deepest part of his lungs before he let it escape. The funeral was tomorrow afternoon. After a brief viewing, the caskets would be closed and the family prayer offered. There were no more chances. Not for him or Jess.

Smoke patted the edge of his dad's casket and dipped his head in solemn tribute to the father he'd never understand. This was the end. The only thing he could think to say was what he'd already told Jess. "I'm keeping the ranch."

Chapter Eighteen

Foot tapping escalated each time Jessie peeked through the wooden blinds in her front room. After a pleasant late lunch with Dakota and Lincoln, he'd driven her back to her place. She knew she should stop snooping, but really?

One glance across the field, and it was easy to see why Smoke hadn't been back for breakfast. He might never come back at this rate. There in all her barely-covered glory, lay that Colby woman, sprawled out and sunbathing in a skimpy bikini on his patio, her dark glasses perched on what undoubtedly was a perky, cute-as-a-button nose.

Darn her. If she turned over one more time on that chaise lounge...

Jessie ground her teeth. Her toes picked up the pace. To make matters worse, Colby had set something to cooking in the Montoya barrel smoker. Smelled like barbequed chicken. Smoke's favorite. How'd she know that? Exactly how close were he and Colby?

Most importantly, how could anyone, even a super model, compete with a nearly naked woman already stretched out in all her glory on Smoke's patio? Colby was built, from what Jessie could see at this distance. Definite 38-Ds. Long, athletic legs that could wrap around a man's hips and make him think he'd gone to heaven. Honey-blonde locks that looked natural. No dark roots. She was perfect, darn her.

Gah! Women! They played so many games, and every last one of them—us—seemed willing to strip to get a man into bed with them. Not like that was what Jessie did with Smoke. Nah-uh. That was different. She'd not only saved herself for him, she loved him, and she knew he loved her. He just hadn't said it yet. But he would.

Fluffy whined at her side. The poor thing kept carrying his rubber ball wanting to play, but Jessie couldn't relax. "I'm sorry," she told him, but as her words tripped over her tongue, they rang false and downright snarky.

Jessie gulped down her jealousy for a woman she didn't really know, and who might be just a good friend of Smoke's come for a visit. There were plenty of women in the military. It could happen.

Yeah, right. She was willing to bet not many G. I. Janes had the lush figure this Colby person had. Tugging the ball out of Fluffy's slobbery mouth, she bounced it into her kitchen and wiped her hand on her jeans.

This day had really gotten out of hand, her emotions, too. Smoke didn't deserve a bitchy woman on his hands or in his bed. She needed to take a break now that the funeral parlor had what they needed. Ethan was in good hands, and there was no way Fernando could get to her unless he was on a plane headed west this very minute. She was absolutely not going to check her voice mail in case that annoying real estate creep had called again. Sheeesh, Jenkins Lassiter had a lot of nerve.

Jessie took a deep breath, her faithful companion again at her side with his tail thumping on the hardwood floor, his bright eyes begging her to come play.

"How about we go for a long walk?" she asked, smoothing her fingers through the silky pompom on his head. "You know, maybe Smoke's right. You do look like a prissy poodle. Let's get you a decent shave and stop dolling you up. Would that make you feel more like a guy dog?"

As if he understood, Fluffy barked, and the decision was made, but...

"Should we change your name, too?" Canting her head, she tried a couple names on for size. "How about Ruffy? You know, something that rhymes with Fluffy, so you won't mind the change? Muffy? Nah. Scruffy? Hmm. Let me think on that one. I know, Tuffy."

She laughed at her silliness which was exactly what she'd needed, a little humor in her crazy mixed-up day. Jessie turned her cell phone on to place a quick call to her other faithful companion, one Lincoln Jefferson Stauffer.

A smile tugged at her lips when she heard his kindly, "I've been hoping you'd call. Where would you like to go now?"

Something was missing when Smoke pulled onto *The Lost Chaparral,* and it wasn't just overarching branches, stately oaks, or red bricks. It was Jess. The woman knew him like a book, and better yet, she still liked him after all these years. Make that loved him. Damned if he understood why.

Jess's one hundred eighty degree change this morning baffled him at first, but he should've known. Her mood swing hadn't a thing to do with missing breakfast or his decision to sell the ranch. He'd pissed her off, and damn it, he should've seen it coming.

Women had a language all their own, but after their night of hot and heavy sex, most especially since Jessie revealed that she'd saved her body and heart for him—duh! He should've been a helluva lot smarter. He should've told her he loved her and asked her to marry him right then and there.

For the first time in forever, he'd had her right where he'd wanted her, those sweet breasts mashed up against him, her arms around his neck, and her green eyes all dreamy. But what'd he do? He'd missed the mark was what. Didn't even come close to a bulls-eye, and him some hotshot sniper.

No. Like some dumb jock, he'd been so caught up in the big picture that he'd missed the close up and personal treasure snuggled in his arms. He talked about selling the ranch, and he'd missed his chance at romance. Worse, he'd made Jessie feel unimportant, and that hurt. He knew what it felt like to be alone and minimized, to not have that special someone at your six.

"Colby?" he called at the front door of the hacienda. His nostrils flared at the delicious aromas in the air. Bacon for sure, but what else? Pork? Chicken? Chocolate? All of the above? He couldn't decide.

Wandering back through the kitchen solved part of the puzzle. The back door was open. Country music along with sunshine spilled inside from the patio, but Colby had been busy. A frosted chocolate cake sat on the counter. His stomach growled.

Palming the screen door open he had to smile. His friend had made herself at home all right. Something tasty was definitely in the smoker, no doubt those two chickens of Jess's. Wearing a sexy sarong over her swimsuit, he guessed Colby had been sunbathing if those pink shoulders were any indication. Her back was to him. The woman had a bottle of beer tipped to her lips and a sensual sway going on. Dancing. No doubt listening to her latest greatest playlist on an iPod or MP3 player tucked—somewhere.

He paused to watch. Colby was a sexy woman. Curvy hips. Blonde. Tanned. Smelling like coconut and lime. Yes, she was gorgeous, but there'd never been anything between him and Colby. She wasn't Jess.

Smoke didn't dare tap her shoulder, not with her Smith and Wesson 22 Victory lying on the patio table beside an empty beer bottle. She wasn't one to keep her weapon handy. If it was out in clear sight, it meant she'd had trouble while he'd been gone, and she'd be quick to draw now.

Colby came with a dangerous startle reflex since she'd come home from the Mideast, so he approached wide to her left, opting to check on whatever was in the smoker instead of tangling with her head-on. Once she glimpsed him out of the corner of her eye, she'd be okay. She'd settle down. God bless the fool who sneaked up on her, thinking he was funny. She had a helluva right hook.

When she stopped swaying, he knew he'd been made, and it was safe to proceed. He lifted the smoker lid and went straight to heaven. Succulent, hickory smoked chicken. Yes!

"You've had company," she said, her dark glasses pulled low on her nose.

"Let me guess. Some silver-haired real estate guy with a big mouth and a death wish. You buried the body behind the barn, right?" A man could only hope.

She pursed her lips but shook her head. "I wish. This is gonna piss you off, so don't go ballistic on me."

What now? He followed Colby off the patio to the southern exposure to his stable where some joker had tagged the red painted wall with a ten-foot purple happy face. No big deal. He didn't like it, but he could live with it. Kids.

"Not that," she bit out, palming the stable door open. "This."

Colby tugged the light on and—

Son-of-a-goddamned-bitch! "Who did this?" he roared, as pissed as he'd ever been. "Do you know?"

Poor Chip! Poor Tango and Brandy, Mesquite and Montana! Smoke couldn't believe his eyes. This was felony animal abuse! Some rat bastard had hacked off their long, flowing manes and tails, leaving jagged spikes and chunks that made them look like crazed punks. Worse were the spray-painted block letters on their sides.

Chip bore the longest word—SORRY—in ugly rainbow caps. Smoke didn't have to see gentle Tango to know he'd find either YOU'LL or BE sprayed there. Sure enough. Line the horses up and he'd get, *'You'll be sorry.'* Ever heard that before? *Damn Lassiter to hell.*

Other filthy words and symbols covered the rest of the mare's rumps and necks. Shit! Smoke kicked at the loose hay on the stable floor, not wanting to bellow because it would scare the already traumatized horses. But God! He clenched his fists, needing to hit something. Someone! Instead he opened the stable doors to trade the paint vapors for fresh air. "Did you see who did this? It was him, wasn't it?"

Colby shook her head. "I'm not sure who *him* is, but I caught three teenage boys in the act. They made enough noise to wake the dead. That's why my pistol. They needed to know I meant business."

"Shit!" he hissed again, smoothing his wide hands over Chip's long face, trying to impart calm into the gentle beast while rage ruled his soul. "Lassiter put them up to this. I know he did."

"Maybe. But I marched them up to the patio," Colby continued in her low and steady voice, the one she used on guys in the field who'd lost their grip and needed a gentle prod to remember who they were and why they were there. "I called the sheriff and I made them call their parents, so they'd know there would be civil charges filed for what their sons did. Those boys know now that they're in deep shit. I told them if they thought I was bad, to wait until you got home, that you were a dangerous Navy SEAL and wouldn't be as kind as I was. I'm surprised you didn't see Sheriff Daley. He just left with them in his squad car."

"Who were they?" Smoke didn't need names to wring their necks. He moved to Tango next, her silky mane cut to the skin. The sweetheart bowed her face into his chest, nickering softly. Damn.

"What's more important is why they did it. Are you listening?"

He looked up from scratching Tango's ears and gave Colby his full attention. "Spill."

"They were paid," she said, handing him a wad of paper. "The ring leader said some guy offered them each fifty bucks to jack you up. They were supposed to torch the stable, but they didn't. The smartass said you were lucky, you got off easy. I told him to shut up or I'd kick his ass."

Smoke snatched the paper out of Colby's fingers, the same gawddamned flyer he'd ripped off

Jess's back door that morning. "I knew it," he seethed. "I'll kill the son-of-a-bitch."

"And I'll be right there with you, brother," Colby said as calm as sin. "You tell me when and where, and you bet your ass I'll be there. We'll nail this Lassiter guy's balls to the barn door and we'll burn the body. They'll never find a trace. You know I will."

And that was the problem. She'd go into hell with him if he asked. Her blind loyalty stopped Smoke dead in his tracks like she probably knew it would. Colby was no dummy, and she was as good a shot with psychological warfare as she was with her semi-automatic M&P10, her rifle of choice.

Smoke stilled the heady scream for blood vengeance boiling up from his soul. No animal should have to suffer like Chip and the mares were. If Jenkins Lassiter wanted a fight, he'd get one. Smoke wouldn't do anything stupid, like going off half-cocked. He wouldn't drag his faithful companion into a battle they couldn't win. No.

He'd be careful. He'd be quick, and he'd be lethal.

He'd be... Smoke.

CHAPTER NINETEEN

"Thank you," Jessie told the pretty dog groomer at the local kennel. "He looks better."

"Fluffy was no trouble at all, and he didn't need much work. Just a little off the top," Angie replied cheerily, her fingers scratching behind Fluffy's ears. "I think he looks better without all the pompoms, don't you? And the leather collar with spikes makes him look like a bad Mama Jama."

Jessie handed over her credit card, smiling because her baby was smiling. Fluffy liked his baths, and all the attention didn't hurt. "I think you're right. Now maybe my friend will stop giving me a hard time. He said Fluffy looks like a girl dog."

"Oh, yeah? Who's your friend?"

Jessie ducked her head into her shoulders, proud and shy at the same time. "Smoke Montoya."

Angie's eyes grew saucer-wide. "Oh, my gosh, is he back in town? Seriously? Why didn't anyone tell me?"

"He came home for his parents' funeral." Jessie didn't want to give up any more dope on Smoke than she had to. It was kind of funny Angie knew him and not her, though. After all, who was the celebrity around here?

"Do you think you could, umm, get me an appointment to see him, or, I don't know, maybe just a couple minutes alone with him? An autograph? Please?"

"Why?" Jessie asked, amazed at the crazy fan-stalking vibes she was picking up from this young woman.

Angie rolled her eyes. "Because he's my hero. Everyone knows what he did for his country, and we're all so proud of him, and, oh, my gosh! The whole town's been waiting for him. I can't believe it. He's finally back! I'd be happy with just an autograph. Would you mind? Could you? Please say yes."

Jessie slanted a suspicious look at her latest Sunnyvale friend. "I don't know. He's a very private man. How do you know him?"

"I don't, but my dad does. Mr. Montoya served with him." Tears glistened on Angie's lashes. "He saved my dad's life, and I promised Dad if I ever—ever—got the chance, I'd kiss his savior and thank him from the bottom of my heart, and I have to. I just have to. If Smoke doesn't want anyone to know he's here, I'll understand, but it'd sure mean a lot to my mom and me if we could just talk with him. You'll ask him, won't you? Please? The next time you see him?"

Jessie's heart swelled with a little more than just pride for her man. It felt more like humility. Smoke Montoya was the real rock star. He always had been. He was the hero the nation should be fawning over. Not her.

"You bet," she promised as she took Fluffy's leash. "I'm sure he'll make time for you. Is it okay if I call you here once I ask him?"

Angie grinned. "Yes. I work Monday through Friday. Oh, thank you. Thank you so much!" She whirled around the counter and surprised Jessie with a hug. And suddenly Jessie was holding a sobbing groomer in her arms. "My dad wouldn't be alive except for Smoke," Angie whispered raggedly. "If he doesn't want to see me, just tell him I'll love him forever for what he did to save my dad. I'll never forget. He'll always be my hero."

Jessie blinked furiously. *He's my hero, too.* "You bet," she promised again.

With Fluffy now Tuffy, she left the good feeling of the groomers behind. Right on schedule, Lincoln pulled his van alongside the curb, the passenger window down. "Are you kids ready to go home?" he asked with a sly smile.

Jessie drew in a deep breath. *Home.* Yes. She was ready. She had a hero to kiss.

Smoke's anger settled to a silent smolder down in his gut. Thankfully, horses had tough hides. Chip's and the mares' skin hadn't been cut, and they weren't bleeding—a damned good thing for three stupid kids. WD-40 eliminated most of the garish spray paint from their sides and flanks. Warm water and a lanolin-based horse shampoo took care of the rest of the blasphemy.

The simple hands-on therapy of grooming these gentle beasts of burden worked wonders on Smoke's soul. The more he brushed and the longer his strokes over patient broad backs and quivering withers, the more his thirst of vengeance against those punks and Lassiter turned into compassion for the horses. Chip and the mares had been sorely abused, yet they hadn't stomped their hooves or screamed for blood. They didn't rant and rave like he had, either. But that day would come.

After he let the horses out into the field, and after they'd all rolled belly-up in the dirt like freshly bathed horses were prone to do, Colby headed back to her barbequed chicken while Smoke went into the house for a shower. By then, he'd worked up a good sweat and he smelled like horse.

A man can scrub pretty damned quickly when he's got a woman on his mind. After Smoke swiped a towel over his shoulders, he let it drop and turned to the steamy mirror. Wiping a path clear of condensation with the back of his hand, he groomed the thickness off his chin until it was more shadow, less beard. He never liked the Taliban trademark. A haircut was overdue, and Colby would no doubt handle that for him, but it could wait. He brushed his teeth and combed his hair, then used just enough gel to spike it.

By the time he was done, the respectable man in the mirror smiled again. Interesting. Smoke took a second look and liked who he saw. A man with a future. He ran a hand over the side of his head, smoothing his hair one last time. College, another thing he and his dad had fought over, was next.

He'd taken quite a few on-line courses while in the Navy. It was time to follow through with a degree. Criminal Law, his first choice. Physical Therapy, his second. The local Veteran's Hospital needed volunteers, and he meant to assist. Vets needed other vets who understood what they'd been through, damn it.

What would Jess say when he told her his plans, that they also included her? He couldn't wait. After one last quick finger-comb, he dropped his dirty clothes down the laundry chute, pulled on a new pair of jeans and stretched into a clean button-up shirt. They were both wrinkled from being left in this duffle bag, but Jess wouldn't mind. He was a guy. What'd she expect?

Smoke still needed to contact his father's lawyer. It was possible he'd been exorcised from Caleb's last will and testament. Like the trouble with Chip and the mares though, that was a problem best left for another day.

The chicken dinner turned out to be good, but he wolfed it down just as fast as he'd run through his shower. The chocolate cake would have to wait. On his way out the door, he strapped on his underarm holster and the nine that went with it.

Smoke hadn't felt the need to wear it until now. If he ran into Lassiter, he meant business. He wouldn't kill the snake, but he would hold him for Sheriff Daley, and he'd sure as hell press charges.

Like a faithful soldier, Colby waited at the front entry, a shitty grin on her face. She'd traded her swimsuit for faded jeans and a plain white T-shirt. No shoes. Still packing her S&W on her hip. "Damn, hot shot. Don't you look dapper?"

"Shut it, Quaid."

She nodded toward Jess's. "I'm not sure she's home yet, but some guy just pulled up. You know anybody in a black SUV? Looks like a Lincoln MKX? Tall fellow? White linen suit?"

"You can tell it's linen from here?" he teased, angling past her to see for himself. "Might be Lassiter. Don't wait up for me."

She thumped Smoke's shoulder on his way out. "Ride easy, sleep hard, big guy."

"Yeah, whatever." Ride easy, nothing. Lassiter had a smack down coming.

"You want me to call the sheriff for backup?"

He glared over his shoulder, "You want to shut up and let me take care of this?"

Colby grinned. "Copy that. Later, Smoke."

He waved her off, not bothering to look behind him. She knew he'd be back.

Cattle were funny animals. Nosy. As Smoke made his way to Jess's back door, several of Ethan's longhorns ambled to the fence line. Watching like busybody neighbors, they followed along, chewing their cud.

"Man, Ethan, what were you thinking, buddy?" Smoke had to wonder. The guy he knew used to be a beer drinking, party animal. Not a rancher. He must've really gotten serious about some gal to have made a risky investment like this.

Smoke didn't run up the back steps this time, just crept up to the house, doubtful Lassiter would be smart enough to watch his back if he'd decided to break and enter. Smoke had dealt with plenty of bullies during his deployments. They were all over-confident blowhards with more mouth than brains.

Scouting the west side of Jess's home and keeping low beneath the kitchen window, Smoke kept one ear tuned for telltale signs of an intruder. For all he knew, that fancy SUV out front might be Jess's. She had the money. She could've gone shopping today.

He entertained that idea until he heard pounding and cursing at her front porch. Moving stealthily to the lilac bush at the corner of the West home, he crouched low and watched.

A stocky, elegantly dressed Hispanic male in an off-white business suit shaded his eyes as he peered through the leaded glass door. "Goddamn it, girl, I know you're in there. Open up, you bitch," he bellowed as he rattled the doorknob.

Cursing Jess was one sure-fire way to get on Smoke's bad side. The predator deep within him strained against its leash at this stranger's brutal language. This had to be Fernando Sonoma, her agent.

He pounded again, hard enough to rattle the windows. "I'm not going back without you, West. You hear me? Get that through your empty head right now. I own your ass, girl. You know I do. Hell, I own your soul!"

Smoke's hand reached automatically for his pistol grip. *You own shit.*

"I know you're in there, and I know you're fucking brother's dead. He can't save you. You're alone and you're out of time. I'll show you who's boss, you bitch!"

And I'll show you dead, Smoke thought to himself, his temper up.

Mumbling under his breath, Sonoma slipped something from an inner jacket pocket. A miniature pry bar? Interesting what some guys carried for protection. Sticking it into the doorjamb, he grunted, and with one hard smack, wood splintered and the latch was sprung.

Hackles lifted up Smoke's spine at the blatant home invasion committed in broad daylight. Sonoma was no more than inside Jess's house, when Smoke followed him inside, silently closing the door behind him. That Fluffy hadn't barked or intercepted the stranger verified what Smoke suspected. Jess wasn't home. Neither was her dog. For not owning a set of wheels, that woman got around.

He breathed a shallow breath of relief until something crashed upstairs, catching his and Sonoma's attention. The noise sounded like it came from Ethan's room. It didn't make sense. If Jess was up there, so was Fluffy. But that dog should've barked by now. What the hell?

An evil glitter shifted over the guy's face as Sonoma strode to the bottom of the staircase, his chin tilted upward and a pistol in his right hand. "There you are, my perfect little whore," he hissed, his hands braced on the banister, his body poised to run. "I knew you were here. Now we'll see just how tough you are. By the time I'm through with you, you'll need some serious plastic surgery. Tell me to contact your lawyer, will you? I don't think so. It's time you paid what you really owe me."

The walls closed in. A familiar red haze shadowed Smoke's view. Others suffered post-traumatic stress for what they'd seen and done. Not Smoke. Not his demons, either. Sonoma had no idea what he'd just released. The evil within Smoke's soul exercised no restraint, when it encountered wounded women and children in danger in far off countries. It meant to kill their aggressors then, and it would kill this guy now. Sonoma should run. The predator was loose.

Smoke rolled the shadowy hulk off his shoulder, needing to exert a modicum of control over his alter ego. This was what made him outstandingly good—and incredibly bad at the same time. He killed without compunction when the circumstance demanded it, but it never came easy. The fight of his life was always an internal struggle. Him against—him, the shadow inside against what little remained of the light he'd been born with.

"Freeze," he growled, his pistol raised while he battled his worst demon for Sonoma's blood. "Raise your hands and kneel. Get down! Now! Before I blow your fuckin' head off!"

Even Smoke's words weren't his, but belonged to the trained assassin prowling beneath his skin. Deep in his heart. The cold-blooded part of him that had no problem sending bastards like Sonoma to meet their Maker. The trained killer with ice in his veins who offered no quarter and accepted no cowardly apology when judgment came due.

Sonoma jerked to attention. A deadly glitter replaced the rabid sparkle in his blacker-than-sin eyes. Raising both hands, he grinned, his gaze locked on something over Smoke's shoulder and—

A blade struck Smoke from behind, scraping past bone and sinew, burrowing deep in his back. He dropped to one knee at the ambush but managed a glimpse of his attacker.

God, not him.

CHAPTER TWENTY

"Hi, I'm Jessie West." She stuck out her hand, hoping the smile she'd pasted on looked more sincere that it felt. Tuffy whined at her feet, eager to make a new friend.

Colby seemed at home standing there in the Montoya entryway with her hand on the doorjamb, almost like she belonged at the ranch. Her jeans and T-shirt looked soft and comfortable. Too soft. Too damned comfortable.

She looked Jessie and Tuffy over, then latched onto Jessie's hand and tugged her inside. "I was wondering when I'd get to meet you. Come on in. You hungry? You want a beer?"

So not what Jessie had expected. "No, umm, thanks. I just wanted to meet you."

"Why me?" Colby trailed into the kitchen. "I'm nothing special."

"Because any friend of Smoke's is a friend of mine," Jessie answered bravely while she followed, Tuffy prancing at her heels. "Sit," she told him, and he obediently dropped to his haunches, still grinning like a happy boy.

It was hard not to notice the way Colby carried herself, her spine erect, her chin held high, and her full breasts filling that tee like a pro. She had that often sought out ultra-feminine, yet ultra-tough mystique going for her. More feminine than Jessie expected from a woman who'd arrived on a motorcycle in leather chaps and jacket. Her blonde hair was fluffed and layered, one side tucked over her ear. No bangs. Extra pretty with a pink kiss from the sun on her cheeks and the tan glow on her arms.

Even when she grabbed a frosty, long-necked bottle from the refrigerator and twisted the cap off, she still looked womanly. Not a guy. Not tough or crass. Still intimidating though, and Jessie needed to put that notion to rest once and for all. She refused to be scared off by any of Smoke's friends, even the women.

"Are you a SEAL, too?" she asked, making herself comfortable on a stool at the Montoya clay-tiled breakfast bar.

Colby snorted. "There aren't any female SEALs," she said evenly, a twinkle in her eye. "Not yet any way. No, ma'am, I'm Army, least I was. Special Forces Recon. Military intelligence ops, not commando like Smoke. He was upfront in all the fighting. I served undercover, mostly at the rear."

"But I thought you worked together?" Jessie interlocked her fingers while Tuffy sprawled on the floor beside her stool, licking his newly shaved belly.

"Sure we did." Colby shrugged like it was no big deal. "SEALs provided oversight for all departments in the sandbox, not just Navy. Some ops required all colors, not just Army green or Navy blue. It's a new world out there."

"Maybe I will have a beer."

Colby returned to the fridge and grabbed another bottle. "Why are you looking at me like that? Not what you expected?" she asked, the beer tapped and on the counter in front of Jessie. Opening a cupboard, she removed a large bowl, then filled it with water. "Come here, baby," she crooned to Tuffy. "Are you thirsty?"

He looked up at Jessie, waiting her cue, his eyes extra bright and shiny as if he were smitten with Colby, too. All Jessie had to do was scrunch her nose, and Tuffy dived in, slurping the water as if he'd been dying of thirst, the traitor. "I thought you'd be, umm, coarse and foul-mouthed, and, I don't know, covered in tattoos and—"

"You thought I'd look like how Hollywood portrays female soldiers in all their action films, huh?" Colby snickered. "All butched-up and needing a shave?"

Jessie giggled, embarrassed but relieved. Colby was easy to talk to. "Yeah, something like that."

"Well, don't feel bad. I knew Smoke had a girlfriend back home, but you're not what I expected, either." Colby upended her bottle and downed the rest of her beer, her slender neck muscles working as she swallowed. The woman was a natural beauty. Full busted. Lush hips. Athletic, tanned, and obviously not worried one bit about calories—or Jessie. "You're not a bitch at all," she offered with a swipe across her mouth and a twinkle in her soft eyes.

"Did Smoke say I was a bitch?" He had his nerve.

Colby giggled. "Of course not, but all the gossip rags out of New York and Hollywood do a good job of brainwashing John Q Public, don't they? I'm supposed to bully men, and you're supposed to eat 'em for breakfast."

"Yeah!" Jessie nearly squealed. "And people are dumb enough to believe the lies." So much of what television and movie screens portrayed was intended to skew the American psyche. To swing it to the left or the right. To suit the behind-the-scenes political agendas. To make some rich jerk richer.

"What's that wonderful smell?" Her stomach growled. It was hard to miss the delightful aroma of smoked chicken in the air and that chocolate cake on the counter. The one slathered in fluffy frosting with a good sized square missing from the center. She couldn't remember the last time she'd eaten what she wanted without counting calories or points or without Fernando looking over her shoulder.

"That's what's left of your chickens." Colby's shoulders shook at what Jessie really hadn't intended as a joke. "Smoke and I had a busy day. First, someone set fire to your chicken coop, which is why we're having drumsticks tonight. He and I put the fire out, but sorry. You lost two birds. I couldn't let them just lay there, could I? We had to eat them. Then, someone worked his horses over while he went into town and—"

"Tango?" Jessie yelped. "What happened?" The news about the chicken coop fire was bad enough but—

"Now hold on. The sheriff's been here. The three idiots who did it are in jail, but not before they'd hacked off the horses' manes and tails. They sprayed paint and stupid words on the poor things, so yeah. It's been a bitchin' day."

Jessie slid off the barstool, her appetite gone. "Can Tuffy stay here? I have to see them. Do you mind?"

Colby leveled a firm hand to her bicep, her forehead wrinkled with worry. "Are you telling me Smoke didn't send you over here? He hasn't talked with you yet? You didn't know about any of this until now?"

Panic tap-danced up Jessie's spine. "No, why?"

Colby cocked her head. "Because he went over to your place an hour ago. Shit. I thought he sent you over here to chat me up. Yes, leave your dog here. Let's go. Now! Move it!"

Chapter Twenty-One

S ulphur and brimstone.

Rancid fumes.

The cloying taste of soot.

Everything Smoke expected to find when he opened one eyelid for the first time in Hell. Rivulets of orange-blue flames raced along the floorboards like crazy skaters on burning ice. *Floorboards in Hell?* Odd, but there those flames were, slipping over a hardwood dance floor like tiny orange ballerinas in blue slippers and bright yellow hats. The dark underworld sizzled and snapped. It hissed whispers. Steaming secrets.

He grunted to make the skaters go away, but they zipped closer, daring to leave the edge of the wall and slide toward him. Taunting him because he couldn't seem to lift his leaden body at the moment. His head either. Much less flick them away with one finger. That was all it would take, but he'd transformed into a sluggish mass that might melt through the wooden floorboards if he didn't figure out what was going on and get his ass out of there. If he didn't remember what happened. Real. Damned. Soon...

A few feet away, Sonoma lay on the floor in the same prone position, staring with lifeless eyes at Smoke, his face pressed to the same hardwood dance floor. A puddle of blood glistened at his throat.

Oh, yeah. I shot him. He won't hurt Jess anymore. Good.

It took a full minute for Smoke to think more clearly. His shot hadn't hit Sonoma because he'd been stabbed the same time he'd fired. So who'd killed the big shot from New York City?

Feet marched by. In shiny leather shoes. With his cheek seemingly plastered to the floor, Smoke peeled his other eye open to see who had the balls to be in this burning house.

Oh, hell. An array of propane tanks stood like plump little soldiers alongside Sonoma's dead body. Across the hall, some silver-haired guy ransacked Jess's room, dumping dresser drawers and tossing her closet. Looking for something, but damned if Smoke knew what she would've kept in her bedroom that was important enough to kill for.

It was Lassiter. What the hell was he looking for?

Smoke should've felt panicky, but he could barely think through the murk swirling in his head. Lifting shakily to his hands and knees, he remembered the knife embedded in his back. Gravity was a killer. The pull of it against the blade when he moved hurt like a mother. He lowered his chin to the slick, red puddle on the floor. No wonder his brain wasn't working. Loss of blood will do that to a guy. But Jess could still be inside. Lassiter might have incapacitated her.

Reaching his gun hand over his shoulder, Smoke shuddered as his fingertips made contact with the blade handle. Shit. It took a minute, but he managed to get a good grip and yanked it out.

Tossing the knife to the floor, he clawed his way up the table in the hall, struggling to his feet. Lassiter had to be stopped, and Jess had to be rescued, and... *holy shit.* Smoke scrubbed a hand over his ribcage, searching for his pistol. He didn't recall holstering the nine, but there it was. Right where it should've been. Lassiter never looked up from his work. He must've thought he had nothing to fear. *Guess again.*

Smoke pulled his weapon up and prepared for one last stand. Jessie's room wasn't burning, not even her bed, but if the rest of the place was on fire, he didn't have much time. These old farmhouses were deathtraps waiting to happen. He could hear the dull roar overhead. The crackle of hungry flames.

Staggering into Jess's room, he shoved his weapon between the shoulder blades of the real estate tycoon ripping her mattress apart. "Where is she?"

Lassiter stiffened. He lifted both arms, her bed sheet still clutched in his fingers, his head cocked to see over his shoulder. "I don't know who you're talking about."

"Like hell you don't. Jessie West," Smoke hissed. The walls breathed in and out. Bending. Bowing. He shook the scary illusion off. "You torched her chickens, you sick bastard, then you sent a bunch of kids to burn my horses. Now, I'm only going to ask you one more time, where is she?"

"Honest, I don't know what you're talking about, Mr. Montoya," Lassiter blathered. "I was walking by when I saw the fire inside the upstairs window. It was that other guy out there who did it, the one in the hall. He had those punks torch your stable then he killed Miss West. I'm sure of it. Why do you think I shot him?"

"So you stabbed me, then shot him?" What a damned liar.

But the floor pitched like the deck of an aircraft carrier in the middle of twenty-foot waves, and Smoke had no choice. He put one hand out to catch his balance. With a queasy whoosh, the room shifted in and out of focus, and suddenly, Lassiter was in his face.

He grabbed Smoke's pistol like he knew what to do with it, but Smoke had been in a few hand-to-hand fights. Punching the older man's gut, he meant to maintain possession of his weapon. Lassiter mashed a palm to Smoke's face, his fingernails digging into his forehead while he reached for the nine.

"Where is she?" Smoke bit out, the barrel of his piece nearly pointed at Lassiter' head. "Tell me and I won't kill you."

With a quick feint, Lassiter eased up, letting Smoke in close enough to knock foreheads. The firearm flew.

"You're too late!" Lassiter bellowed. "She's at your ranch with that ditsy blonde biker chick. The cabbie dropped her and her stupid dog off an hour ago. Don't think I haven't been watching you for a long time. I always get what I want."

Growling like an old man, he raked his fingernails over Smoke's face, tearing at his nose and into his upper lip. But he missed Smoke's eyes, and with that, he missed his last chance.

Lifting an arm, Smoke elbowed him hard, forcing him back a foot. Lassiter sucked in a groan, but with his hands freed, Smoke curled a fist and hammered Lassiter straight in the face, once. Twice. Then a third time.

The man fell backward onto Jess's bed, but there was no stopping Smoke. That fierce beast inside had leapt to life again. It wanted blood, and Smoke was on board with that. It dragged Lassiter up off the mattress only to knock him down. Drag him up. Knock him down. Again and again. Blood. It wanted blood and the crunch of Lassiter's nose and teeth only fueled its appetite for more.

By the time Lassiter stopped flailing, he was nearly unconscious. The beast inside Smoke settled, mostly because the last of his strength was spent. The con artist moaned, but if he stayed in the house, he'd burn to death. Why Smoke cared what happened to Lassiter, he hadn't a clue. Circling one arm around the murderer's neck, he dragged the guy into the hall.

Smoke should've known better, though. He should've dropped Lassiter and run for his own life. He should've saved himself and let that bastard reap what he had coming to him. Because the signs were everywhere. Slithering flames along the low edge of the baseboards. Inky, black smoke tumbling down the stairs like an ungodly waterfall. *Thump. Thump. Thump.* Orange tongues licking up the walls, hungry for sustenance. The stifling kiss of a closed-up, oxygen deprived fire that needed to breathe. The long, black fingers beckoning him to stay. To burn.

The second Smoke cracked Jess's front door, he shoved Lassiter out first. But he was too late. The house behind Smoke sucked in an almighty inhale and—

WHOOSH! It blew him away.

CHAPTER TWENTY-TWO

"Hurry," Jessie urged while she ran, her hamstrings on fire as much as her house. But Smoke was in there. She knew it with every beat of her pounding heart. He'd gone inside to save her, and he wouldn't stop until he did. He'd die for her, and that was not going to happen.

"You take the front. I'll go in back," Colby ordered, her pistol drawn as they hit the edge of the lawn in record time. Where she came up with that weapon, Jessie didn't have time to care.

Ethan's longhorns stood at the fence line, while Jessie ran around her house, fear a living lump in her throat. Adrenaline gave wings to her feet.

When the second story windows burst outward, raining a shower of wicked glass shards, Jessie ducked and kept going.

It's called back draft, when a burning building finally inhales what it craves, sucking in oxygen to feed the fire in its gut before it blows itself and the combustibles caging it, to smithereens. The ensuing explosion rocked the earth, knocking her to her hands and knees. She covered her head and face with her arms, while her home belched fire and debris, glass and heat, out the front door and every window.

"Smoke!" she screamed, her lungs on fire, the pungent stench of propane on the wind.

Another blast reverberated from deep inside her house. Then another. Ribbons of inky black trickled over her face. Into her eyes. It couldn't end. Not like this! She crawled around the corner of her house to the lawn where a smoldering, blackened body lay with one hand raised. The horrific irony was not lost on her. Smoke was—smoking.

"Here," his ragged voice declared. "Jess. I'm... over here."

She scrambled to him as quickly as she could make her arms and legs work. Cradled him. Cried over him, her voice oddly weak in her head. "I'm here, baby. I'm here."

He looked so bad. His clothes were scorched and shredded. Blood stained his chest. He coughed and gagged, his eyes rolling back in his head.

"Stay with me," she crooned, her hand cupping his bloodied jaw. "You're hurt real bad, Smoke, but help's coming. I promise," she lied, big tears blinding her vision and spilling onto his face. "Don't you dare leave me again."

"Hurt... you..." he ground out through cracked, bloodied lips, his cheeks and forehead blistered and blackened.

"I'm not hurt," she whimpered. *But you are.* "Please don't talk. Save your strength."

He lifted a shaking palm to cup her cheek. "Never... hurt you... again."

She bowed her forehead to his, needing him to think of himself for a change. "Don't worry about me. I'm fine. It's you who's hurt."

"And you." A gentle hand skimmed over her back as Colby knelt at her side. "Helps on its way, kids, but you're making this hard. Let me see what's going on." She logrolled Smoke to his side. "Stay still, buddy. You're both bleeding, but I don't have enough pressure bandages on me to save both of you."

"No, I'm not bleeding. I'm fine," Jessie insisted. "Save him. Please Colby. Not me."

"We'll see." Wasn't that what all parents told their kids when they couldn't or wouldn't commit?

"W-what's wrong?" Jessie asked, her voice oddly detached, the world fading.

"Knife wound," Colby bit out. The woman was an efficient workhorse. She ripped Smoke's shirt open and pressed a large square bandage to his back. But even she looked hazy while she slapped another pressure bandage into the crook of his neck. "Hold his hand, honey. Squeeze it as tight as you can. Keep him awake, while I work on you. Talk to him," she said as she made Jessie lay alongside Smoke.

"Work on me?" That didn't make sense. "W-why?" Finally prone, Jessie interlocked her fingers with Smoke's, fighting to keep the shadows at bay.

Colby didn't answer, but scarier was that Smoke hadn't said another word, just laid there blinking at the sky. Jessie tugged his hand to her lips and kissed his bloodied knuckles, needing him to want to live. After all he'd sacrificed for country and family, he deserved a long life filled with peace and happiness and—

God! Please let him live!

Colby hovered between them like an angel, her blonde hair hanging over her forehead into her face. Working fast. Biting her bottom lip. Her bloodied fingers flew back and forth and back and... forth... until... Jessie couldn't keep track. She was lightheaded and... drifting. Drifting...

The world turned fuzzy gray until Colby snapped back into view. "Keep talking," she urged, a quiet demand in her somber voice.

"Save him. Only him. He's the real hero, not me," Jessie pleaded, her heart focused on the man she loved more than life itself. She curled to her side, needing to see Smoke, but Colby pushed her flat to her back.

"Stay still," she murmured, pressing her hand hard into Jessie's side. "Helps coming, but you've got to hold still. Talk to Smoke. That's all you have to do, honey. Just talk to him and lie still until the paramedics get here. Pour your heart out. You love him, don't you? Then tell him everything you were never brave enough to tell him before. He needs to hear your voice now, sweet thing. Don't let him down. Please? For Smoke? Be braver than you've ever been."

Jessie stared at the sky while she sobbed and cried, "I love you, Smoke Montoya. I need you so bad, and all of Sunnyvale needs you, too. You just don't believe it because of your parents, but they were wrong, and I want babies, damn it. Your babies. I want a life. With you. Only with you."

Her strength sapped, it took everything just to turn her head to see if he was still with her or not. A funny cloud hovered over them, a gray cloud with piercingly bright silver edges. A cloud that reached down to her until she couldn't see though it anymore.

"Promise me," she whispered, her voice gone lighter than air. Lighter than her. The gray cloud hovered, its cool moist darkness at her lips. On her cheeks. Covering her eyes.

The wish wheezed out of her. "Promise, Smoke. Promise you'll tell me... you love me... once... before I... die..."

Smoke heard Jess murmuring at his side, but he couldn't make his neck work to look at her or his mouth to answer. No strength responded to his call-to-arms. No meaningful words jumped to his lips. Nothing rolled off his tongue, but drool. And blood. He sputtered and choked the thickness of it out of his windpipe.

"How you doing, big guy?" Colby asked, her bright and smiling face overhead, the wide Texas sky behind her on what should've been a picture-perfect day. Not this nightmare.

She glanced toward the road and he watched her mouth moving, her head bobbing like she agreed with him, only he hadn't said anything. He just wanted to hold Jess. To wrap her up tight in his arms and comfort her, but his hand felt cold and empty, bereft of its one and only lifeline.

She'd let him go. She was dying, and he wasn't there for her. He'd been too late to save his parents, and now, too late for her. Panic climbed up his throat, tearing at him like he'd swallowed a handful of razors. He stabbed Colby with all the fury in his eyes. *'Please help me.'*

But she was talking to someone else. Not paying attention.

He growled for all he was worth. *'Help. Me!'* he commanded mentally. Prayerfully. *'God, please help me help Jess.'*

Suddenly Colby's gaze shifted. She smiled down on him with that same sad smile he'd seen too many times in the past. In the high Hindu Kush where men died far from home and loved ones. In squalid jungles of South America when heroes fell in the line of duty.

His heart dropped into that hollow cavern deep in his soul, the one where only he and his demon lived. "Please..." he croaked, his strength waning, his final fight nearly done.

Colby wiped her eyes, but finally did what he needed. She cupped Jess's limp hand into his bigger palm, the hand that should've kept her from dying.

He tugged her tiny fingers to his lips and promised what was left of his heart. "Love... you... Jes-s-s-s..."

CHAPTER TWENTY-THREE

Smoke woke up early the second day after the blast. He'd survived, but he still had a mission. Colby had assured him Jess was out of ICU, so today was the day. They'd gotten separated in the hustle of paramedics saving their lives. He'd lost most of his hair, one eyebrow, some scalp, his hearing in one ear, and a lot of blood in the explosion. But the secret most folks didn't know was SEALs were too mean to die. Death didn't get to come aboard without asking permission first.

The emergency surgery that had repaired a few vital arteries was behind him, and yeah, Smoke knew he should've been lying flat on his back, healing, following doctor's orders, and all that rot. But some things couldn't wait. He was damned well going to toddle on over to see Jess.

Toddle. Ha. There he was, creeping along like a weak old man in a walker, half afraid he'd fall if he lifted his feet too far from the floor. His IV tree tagged along behind him. And the nurse who held it. Colby was there. Other folks, too. He didn't know why he was suddenly leading a parade. The farther he walked, the more folks gathered at his six.

"Is my ass hanging out?" he asked Colby out of the corner of his mouth.

She tipped backward enough to leer at his butt, her brows lifted in mischief. "Yeah. It's kind of cute, too. I've never seen this side of you, big guy. You've got a tat? Good one. You want me to cover it up?"

He spiked as mean a brow as he could muster, not that one scorched brow on an ugly face would frighten a gal as tough as Colby.

"Damn it, I don't have a tat on my ass. It's a burn. Cover it up," he growled, still not able to twist and turn to take a look at his butt like he wanted.

Smoke had his hands full just holding onto his spiffy, aluminum walker. His back was stiff and sore as hell, and his ears were prone to ringing. He fell down a lot more than he'd admit. Funny girl Colby had brought four pink tennis balls to cover the stoppers on his walker. Shit. He looked like an old man. Felt like one, too.

She laced her arm through his, her palm on his bicep. "I'm teasing, big guy. Your ass is covered, and we're almost there."

"Who are all these people?" He had to ask.

The cheerful nurse with the IV tree mumbled behind him, something about, "...once you get to your girlfriend's room."

"Heh?" he asked Colby, cupping a hand to his one good ear.

"She said you sure have a lot of friends," Colby said that loudly and proudly and, damn it. Something was up, and Smoke didn't like it. Not one bit. Jess's room was a lot farther away than he'd expected.

"Will there be enough room for all these people when and if we get there?" he muttered at Colby. "Shit, where're you taking me? To Cowboy Stadium?"

Colby whispered so low he could barely hear what she said, but he refused to ask her to repeat herself. It only made him look sillier than he already did.

He toddled around the corner, past a pair of open chapel doors, then past another couple empty rooms. Finally, Colby stopped. He shuffled his feet, needing to sit before he fell down. "We there?"

She lifted her brows and smiled as she palmed the door opened wide. "We're there, big guy."

"Don't yell at me. I heard you," Smoke groused, peering around the door, needing to see the lovely woman he thought he'd lost.

Poor Jess lay still on the bed, pale and fragile. One arm was wrapped in white gauze from her fingers to her shoulder, and a bandage was plastered to her forehead. She waggled her fingers at him, the sweetest smile on her pretty face. "Hey. How are you doing?"

He shuffled as fast as his damned stiff legs could get him to her side but broke down when he buried his face against her shoulder. "Jess," he blurted out, his tears falling like rain. He just stood there, bowed into her and cried like a damned baby.

Her fingers smoothed lightly over his tender scalp. "I thought I lost you," she sobbed, her lips to his good ear. "I love you so much."

That was precisely what Smoke needed. He let go of the walker and leaned into her quaking body, nuzzling into the crook of her neck, inhaling her scent into his lungs again. "I've got you, baby," he declared even as he choked, his poor, smoke damaged lungs as ragged as his heart, "and I'm never letting you go."

"I've got you, too," she murmured breathlessly. "I love you, Smoke. I always have. I always will."

"I know," he growled, "because... well, I've loved you forever, Jessie West."

She lifted her arm and drew him into her warm embrace. "I knew it," she whispered against his ear. "I always knew you loved me."

He had to wonder. If they'd had this conversation back when, would it have changed where they were today? Would she have still left Sunnyvale? Would she have needed that drastic escape from the grief of losing her parents if he'd been brave enough to share his heart? Was he just like his damned father? Too proud to give the one person who loved him the most what she'd needed to survive?

He gulped at his younger man's arrogance and ignorance. "You're going to marry me, Jessie West," he growled softly, "and we're going to start making babies as soon as you're up to it. Do you hear me?"

The most radiant smiled blossomed over her face. "As soon as *I'm* up to it?"

He shrugged, casting a quick glance in the direction of his groin. "Well, yeah. You know me. I'm always up for it. Least I used to be."

The crowd at the doorway chuckled and clapped like nosy neighbors. They'd heard everything he'd said. "Damn it. These folks keep following me. I can't shake them."

"Have a seat, Smoke," Colby urged as she pulled a chair alongside Jess's bed. "Sit down and be quiet. This town has something to say to both of you."

"This town? What do they want?" Now that he was facing them, he saw a few people he knew. Smitty. Jared. Both dressed in suits. That couldn't be good. He sank in relief to the chair, Jess's tiny little hand snug in his, finally where it belonged.

Just seeing her again did his heart good. The last thing he'd remembered was the paramedics lifting her onto a gurney and taking her away. She'd taken a nasty shower in shattered glass when her house exploded. She'd lost a good deal of blood and suffered a few cuts. The sword-like shard that pierced her lung caused the most trouble. It never slowed her down, though. The crazy woman never felt it, just crawled to his side, trying to save him while he'd thought he was saving her. It was funny what lovers did for each other.

"Smoke Montoya." Damned if Jared didn't start off with a big shitty grin on his mustached lip. "This room's too damned small."

Smoke shrugged. "It was fine 'til you guys showed up."

More chuckles. More clapping. Smoke rolled the pinch out of his neck. They thought he was being funny when he wasn't. This was starting to feel like some kind of a presentation. Shit. And there he was in a hospital gown and powder blue socks, wishing everyone would leave. "What's this all about, Jared? Why are you and your friends here?"

The man had two brows he could actually waggle. "Because they're your friends, too, and because Sunnyvale would like to thank you and Miss West..." He paused for attention. "...for what you both did to help apprehend Jenkins Lassiter. If it hadn't been for you kids, he'd still be pushing folks off their property and out of their homes. Your place wasn't the only fire we've had recently, and I'm glad you're sitting down, Smoke, cuz there's something else you need to know."

A shiver of premonition breathed its icy breath down the back of Smoke's neck. He'd never felt more exposed and vulnerable. His palms itched for a good handgun to make every one back off. His gut clenched with that creepy sensation a sniper gets when he knows something wicked's on its way. With Jessie's fingers intertwined with his, he held his breath and waited.

"You asked why your mom and dad weren't in their fallout shelter when the tornado hit. That got me to thinking. With all we now know about Lassiter's dirty work, I met with Sheriff Daley over at Sam's Donut Shop this morning, and he agrees with me."

"What? That Sam's donuts are mighty good?" somebody in the crowd joked.

"And his coffee's better?" some other wise guy quipped.

Teeters rippled through the crowd. "Yeah, yeah, I know what you're all thinking. Cops and donuts, ha ha, but you'll be glad to know by the time I thought of it, Sheriff Daley has already opened an official investigation into your parents' deaths, Smoke. That F5 might have been an unfortunate coincidence that covered up what really happened the day they died. Did you ever wonder why there was a black Caddie in your neighbor's field? I didn't until this mess happened. Anyway, the sheriff won't rest until he's sure of their real cause of death. He and I both think Lassiter was behind it. He may be looking at the electric chair."

"Bastard should," Smoke muttered, lifting Jess's fingertips to his lips, wanting everyone to leave, so he could tuck her into his body where she belonged. Hell, so he could crawl into bed beside her and kiss every last one of her hurts away. Maybe then he'd get another decent night's sleep.

"And another thing..." Jared turned his attention to Smitty, his hair freshly combed and slicked back. "Mr. Ferguson has something to say."

Bingo. Presentation time.

"Ahem." Smitty flushed a deep crimson at the spotlight he found himself under. "I told you I would take care of you, and I am a man of my word, Mr. Montoya. Yesterday I sold the lumber from your trees to a fine cabinet-maker in Houston. He was very excited to have such beautiful, old lumber, and he paid top dollar. Here's the check along with a small token of *your* town's gratitude," he emphasized, "*your* town of Sunnyvale, Texas, where we take care of our own, and where we honor our heroes."

Oh, God. Not that.

But yeah. Exactly that.

Smitty presented an envelope and a polished, beveled oak plaque. Thick. Beautiful grain. Burned into the center of the platter-sized piece of wood, right below the golden eagle, anchor and trident, was this inscription:

To Smoke Montoya
Gunner's Mate Second Class
United States Navy
Proud Son and Hero of Sunnyvale, Texas
With our undying respect and appreciation
For battles fought
For unknown hardships and sacrifices endured
For lives saved
Thank you for being that guy

Smitty beamed. "I made this from one of your trees."

Like that helped a man regain his control. Smoke eased his hand from Jess's before one tear fell, a damned lump in his throat at these unexpected sentiments.

"And another thing..." Jared just wouldn't shut up. He tugged a young woman out of the crowd to his side. "This gal has something to say while you're still here where we can find you."

That smartassed remark elicited another round of chuckles. The gal shrugged her shoulders, waved a dainty little flutter at Jess, and turned an even brighter shade of red than Smitty. She swallowed hard. "Mr. Montoya, I'd, umm, like to be the first to kiss the hero of Sunnyvale, if you, umm, wouldn't mind. Just a teensy little one. On your cheek. Please?"

Colby muffled a grunt from where she stood behind him, but what was a guy to do? He beckoned the young thing on over to get the deed over with. The moment she leaned in, there, with every one watching, she twined her fingers around his neck and placed her feather soft lips on his cheek like she'd promised. Easing back, her shining eyes scrolled to Jess. "I wasn't going to kiss his mouth, Miss West. That's for you to do later. Thank you, Mr. Montoya. You're a good sport."

She stepped away and drew in a deep breath, then turned back with bright eyes. "In case you're wondering why I had to do that, you're my second favorite hero. The first one's my dad. You saved his life in Asadabad, Kunar Province, Afghanistan. My mom and me can't ever thank you enough for making sure he came back home to us. And I told him if I ever—ever—was lucky enough to meet you..." Her voice rapped up higher and tears dripped down her face, but she didn't wipe them away, just kept going, breaking his heart all over again. "...I'd kiss you and tell you thank you so, so much. You'll never know what giving my dad back to us means. You saved me that day, too." She swallowed hard, her voice squeaky. "You really did. His name's Ronald Preston, and he'd really like you to come over for dinner some night."

Smoke nodded, remembering that mountain rescue, the Army squad pinned down, and those poor damned guys facing a rough retreat with no way to go but back up those steep cliffs, getting peppered all the way. "You're Ronnie G's daughter? How's he doing? Is he walking yet?"

Ronnie G, the G for Goddamn. Preston earned that handle the time he'd run into a blind alley, guns blazing to rescue his fellow soldiers. There was a time he'd been one tough son-of-a-bitch.

"He'll never walk again, but he's got a service dog now, and he's doing better every day," she said, wringing her hands. "Please come visit. It'd mean the world to Mom and me, too."

Smoke gestured her to come back. "It's a deal," he said quietly, just between him and her as he drew that girl back down to his level until they bumped foreheads "You tell Ronnie to name the day and time, and I'll be there. What's your name?"

She scrunched her shoulders, her gaze drifting over to Jess. "I'm Angie, and I groomed Jessie West's poodle. That's how we met."

"For your information, Fluffy is now Tuffy, and you'd better be careful. He's got spikes on his collar," Jess said softly but proudly. "And he's full of attitude."

Smoke pressed a heartfelt kiss to Angie's forehead before he let her get away. "Your dad's a damned good man. You tell him I said so. Tell him I'm bringing the beer to that picnic, and he'd better help me drink it."

"One more thing," Jared piped up when Angie stepped back into the crowd, wiping her face.

Oh God, what now?

Damned if the governor of Texas didn't lean his Stetson covered head through the doorway, a young man who looked to be his assistant right behind him.

Smoke rolled his eyes at Jess, their hands once again clenched tight. *What now?*

"Is this him? Is this our guy?" Governor Logan asked as he removed his hat.

"Yes, sir," Jared answered.

Smoke struggled to come to attention while keeping his rear covered. He didn't get far. The governor motioned him to sit back down, and he was glad to obey.

"Smoke Montoya," Governor Logan said, his hand outstretched, "it's an honor to meet you, son. I hear you've had a couple exciting days."

Smoke returned the handshake. "Guess you could say that. Thank you, sir."

It was difficult to miss the soft glint in the man's appraising eye as they scrolled over Smoke's obvious condition and over to Jess's. "Howdy, ma'am," he said gently. "This great state is proud of our favorite son here. You must be proud of him, too."

Smoke blinked as he turned to face Jess. She had that look on her face, that little girl look of total adoration, the one from their rodeo days, when she'd win a trophy or a ribbon. Her eyes were red-rimmed, teary, and tired. She needed rest as much as he did. He'd been so scared he'd lost her after the explosion at her house, but there she was, smiling anyway.

He lifted her hand to his mouth and kissed the back of it, pouring every bit of his tattered soul into that kiss, needing her in his bed and every coming day of his life.

She mouthed a teary '*I love you*' that pinched his heart. He desperately wanted the governor to take all of these folks out the door with him and just—go.

But Governor Logan strode over to Jess's bed and thrust a second cowboy hat into Smoke's hand. "Let's see if I can't make some of those bad memories go away. Gunner's mate second class Smoke Montoya, on behalf of the great state of Texas, I present you with a very small token of our appreciation for your particular brand of steadfast loyalty and American service. It's just a hat, and I know you've received bigger and better awards from the Navy, but this one's from us, son. As God is my witness, I hope you'll decide to stay where you belong from now on. In Texas."

Smoke nodded one quick, short affirmative to the man. "Yes, sir, I plan to," he replied, his voice hoarse and unsteady, not his style at all.

The governor beamed, his hand extra gentle on Smoke's wrist instead of on his burned shoulder. "Go ahead. Put it on."

Reluctantly, Smoke fingered the crease and tucked the hat over his shorn scalp. It fit perfectly.

So did the manly wink from Jared across the room. He had to be the guy behind all this pomp and circumstance.

"There now. You look like one of us again." A round of applause circulated the room, but the governor quelled the racket with one upraised palm. "Now listen everybody, because this next announcement's official. You're all hereby invited as my personal guests to the state capital." He faced Smoke with somber attention. "You too. I want you at the dedication of the bronze statue in your name. You're our hero, and we want the world to know it."

Smoke shook his head, overwhelmed. A bronze statue to honor him? *What a waste.*

Doffing the hat, he set it on the end of Jess's bed, then held up his free hand to speak. "Sir. Good folks of Sunnyvale. I appreciate the sentiments, I do, but I'm no hero. Honest. I'm still alive..." He paused, his heart stuck in this throat and tears he didn't want to shed, imminent. He swallowed hard before he could go on. "If you don't mind me saying so, the real heroes are the guys and gals who didn't come home. They're like Angie's dad, the ones who lost their arms or legs or their minds. You're making a mistake honoring me. Honor them instead. Please."

The governor lifted his interlocked fingers to his lips, his gaze intent on Smoke. "But the statue's already cast with your face. We've just been waiting for you to come home to give it to you."

Jared's chin lifted, and Smoke wasn't sure if it was pride or censure glimmering in his friend's eyes. He was most likely the driving force behind the statue, too. He'd probably done a lot of work and contacted state legislators and donors to make it happen. It still didn't matter. None of it did. War wasn't about praise and glory. Those things weren't real, but death and sacrifice were. What Angie and her mother suffered sure as hell was.

Damn. Smoke dropped his chin to his chest, fighting for composure and remembering every last friend and teammate he'd lost to combat-related injuries. To suicide. To despair. To divorce or to being deserted or forgotten. To homelessness. That crap was real. He didn't want to turn down a gift from Texas, but neither did he want honor or praise, while other good men and women suffered in silence.

Smoke just wanted anonymity, to be left alone. To sleep with his arms wrapped around Jess every night for the rest of his life. To plant babies in her belly and raise 'em up to be as strong and pretty and sassy as their mama. To reach out to every last, lost warrior and bring them home. He wanted a country that sacrificed for their military members as much as those guys and gals had sacrificed for Americans.

At last he raised his head, his mind made up. "I don't know what to tell you, Governor Logan. I'm proud as hell of Texas, and I intend to stay, but I don't want a statue. I'm no hero, sure as hell not someone like Chris Kyle. He was the legend. I was just doing my job, sir. Surely you understand."

United States Navy Chief Petty Officer Chris Kyle, was the real American hero from Texas. Everyone knew that.

A look passed from Governor Logan to Smoke. The governor was an older soldier from a different war. He'd also served, his time spent in the jungles of Vietnam. The harsh realities of Tet and far off places like Quang Tri reflected in his quiet gaze. Smoke knew because he'd studied the man before he'd mailed his absentee ballot in the last election. Logan was a Texas boy, born and raised, and Smoke had known precisely the caliber of man he'd wanted at the helm of his state.

A quiet murmur shifted through the gathering. "Well, damn it son," Jared quipped, his eyes glistening and his voice extra gravelly. "You're quite the man. Governor, would it be okay with you if we changed the words on the plaque to that bronze memorial? You could do that, couldn't you?"

The governor's eyes narrowed. "What would you like it to say, Smoke?" he asked quietly. "You tell me what words to put on it, and I'll make it happen."

Smoke lifted to his feet, his hand outstretched to seal the deal with his governor. "'Remember them'. That's all, sir. In my opinion, we need to remember every last one of them every single day. They'd like that."

Chapter Twenty-Four

Damn. Colby had certainly done a bang-up job getting the hacienda ready for the next generation of Montoyas. By the time Smoke brought Jess home from the hospital, she'd already moved his parents' furniture into an on-site storage container where he could sort through it another day. By the looks of the place, she'd also brought in a team of painters. Where Colby got the money to do all she'd done, Smoke had no idea, and he knew better than to ask. She'd never tell. But damn. It looked like the entire place had been re-carpeted, re-painted, and wasn't that a kick to come home to?

Bamboo blinds replaced the drapes throughout. Caroline's quaint southwestern motif had been artfully converted to rustic modern, Colby's term for the leather recliners, the big screen TV, and a damned nice gun safe in the far corner of the front room. She'd left Caleb's cowboy hat hanging on the hook by the front door, waiting for another hard day's work.

Smoke swapped it out with his Stetson.

"Your room's ready," Colby said as she led the way down the hall toward what had once led to his bedroom on the left, his parents' on the right. Not anymore. When she palmed the door to the master suite open, she revealed another complete make-over. A king size bed now graced the opposite wall, its headboard a massive display of polished branches with knots in them as big as a man's fist and—

All that wood *was* oak.

"Is that my trees? Did Smitty do this?" Smoke had to ask.

Colby shrugged. "You know, he wouldn't say, but I'm almost a hundred percent sure this bed used to stand out in your front yard. You like?"

"Wow," Jess breathed as she limped into the room alongside Smoke. "It's beautiful."

That it was, and better yet, there was nothing left in the room to remind Smoke that his parents had once slept there. Which was sad, but necessary. Caleb and Caroline had their chance. Their time was over, but Smoke's and Jess's time was just beginning.

But further explanations could wait. Jessie was tired. Once he got her up and into the football-field-sized bed, Smoke pressed a kiss to her forehead and told her to, "Get some rest. I'll be in after I talk to Jared."

"Promise?" she asked drowsily.

"Promise," he whispered as he closed the door and retraced his steps to the front room. "You've been busy," he told Colby.

"Yeah, well..." She looked him straight in the eye. "This place needed a makeover."

That it did. Smoke strolled through the kitchen. "I wondered where they went," he said when he spied his mother's prized Talavera planters out on the patio. The kitchen looked pretty much the same, only the dishes, silverware, and appliances had been updated. "You didn't have to do all this," he said quietly.

"Yeah, I did. A gay and his gal need a fresh start. That's all this is. You let me room with you for years, so put a sock in it. It was my turn to pay it forward."

"Yes, but—"

"No, buts. Consider it my wedding present to you and Jessie. I'll be gone by then, and..." She turned away from him to look out the sliders, her words hanging as she stared off into space.

"Where will you go?"

Her lips twisted with what was either discouragement or cynicism, with Colby it was sometimes hard to tell. "Boston," she blew out on a drawn out sigh. "Eventually, I'll have to go back to Boston."

Which didn't seem to make her happy, but Smoke let it slide. She'd tell him when she was ready.

"So what's next?" Colby asked, changing the subject as she reconnected, just a hint of wistfulness still glimmering in her eyes. "Is Jessie going to stay here with you or—"

"Here," Smoke answered clearly. Succinctly. There was no question about it, Jess would stay where she belonged. With him. "She heard back from her lawyer late last night. Martelli had no trouble getting her out of her contracts, not after the two attempts on her life."

"Why do I get the feeling there's a but to that story?" Colby asked. Damn, her instincts were as good as ever.

"Because Jess is good at what she does," he answered grumpily. "Martelli no more than ended his call when she got an offer from one of her biggest clients. I thought they'd all leave her alone after what happened, but you know how it goes."

Colby's eye lit with mischief. "She really is a big star. You know that, don't you?" she asked in her how-stupid-can-you-be voice.

Now it was Smoke's turn to stare out the window. "Yeah, but these guys want her bad enough to let her run her own photo shoots, schedules, and damn. They're flying out next month to sign her up for a couple more years."

"She wants to?"

Smoke nodded. Of course, Jess wanted this contract. For the first time in her career, she could set her limits, and there'd be no crooked agent breathing down her neck, pushing her to do more with less—clothing, that is. "It's perfect for her," he told Colby, though it felt more like he was trying to convince himself. "It's a new makeup and fragrance line. *Western Stars*. She'll be the face every young girl wants to be. Like Taylor Swift. She'll be famous the world over."

"You don't sound happy about it," Colby said as she knuckle bumped his bicep, jolting him out of his not-as-thrilled-as-he-should-be reverie. "Oh, wah, wah, wah. Smoke Montoya's going to marry the country's sexiest fashion model and live happily-ever-after. How awful. Trust me, you'll survive, big guy. You ever think of buying that spread west of you?"

"Hardy's place?" Smoke canted his head, considering it now.

Colby snorted. "Hell, yeah. Between your place, Jessie's, and that parcel to the west, you kids'll have enough land to build a damned fine hide-away. By the way, your dad's lawyer called this morning. He said you need to call him as soon as you can. Something about the number of barrels coming out of your next dozen rigs."

"I don't have a dozen rigs," Smoke said as he held up one finger. "One. Just one."

"Not anymore," Colby teased. "Face it, Smoke. Your life's changing. Embrace it. Hell, run with it. You and Jessie will go far together."

And wasn't that the truth? The way it had always been. Every step, every battle, every dream and every nightmare Smoke had ever had, they'd all been steering him back to Jess. Because Colby was right. He and Jess would go far.

Smoke turned back the way he'd come. "I've got to go," he told the girlfriend who'd never be his wife or his lover. Her turn would come one day, but it wasn't now and it wasn't here with him.

"Ride easy. Sleep hard," Colby answered from the kitchen behind him.

It was true. Lassiter hadn't stopped them. In fact, Sheriff Daley now had enough evidence to send the real estate mogul to prison. The murderer had finally admitted he'd been after the deed to the West family farm in Jess's room that day. But all he'd found were Ethan's pedigree charts on the longhorns. Texas longhorns.

Smoke paused in his old room long enough to locate a couple packages he'd stored, then fast-footed it to his new room door to watch. Just to watch. There Jess lay where he'd left her, sound asleep, her clasped hands drawn up alongside her cheeks as if in prayer.

Stealthily, Smoke stashed his packages beside the bed, doffed his clothes, and climbed in behind her. Groaning, she tucked her soft, warm backside inside the curve of his very wide-awake body.

Healing took time, but there was no better place for it to begin than here in this bed.

My bed. With me.

Lifting her ebony tangles, he burrowed his nose into the nape of her neck, hoping to entice her to wake up. Inhaling the fragrance of chocolaty orange in his brand new world, Smoke licked his lips at the promise of eating breakfast.

The moment was now. He'd go up in flames if he didn't make his intentions official. The scent of her clean hair, the touch of her satin skin against his chest and arms and legs worked his last nerve. Arching forward he bumped his hips to her butt to get her attention. She already had his. "Hey Jess, you really going to sleep all day?"

"Maaaay-beeee," she grumbled, her voice hoarse but her backside still touching him.

As he brought one arm over her to place his first gift in front of her pretty nose, Smoke said what he intended to say every day for the rest of his life, "I love you, beautiful."

Opening her sleepy eyes, Jess cupped the small black velvet box in both hands. "What's this? Oh, my gosh, Smoke?"

He loved the sexy trepidation in her tone, the way she asked when she knew damned well what was in that jeweler's box. "It's the rest of my life," he murmured, rubbing his nose up the side of her face and into her hair. Breathing. Just breathing. "Open it."

Shifting to her butt, Jess dragged the sheet up to cover her naked self. Silly woman. That scrap of cloth wouldn't last long. She bit down on her bottom lip, trembling, her dark hair spilled over her shoulders like a silky cape, her gaze riveted on the box. "For me?"

He nudged her hip, his arm protectively around her. "Yes, for you. Everything I am is because of you, Jess. Now stop playing around and open it."

She nodded, drew in a deep breath and snapped the velvet lid up. Inside rested the blood red Burma ruby he'd spent tens of thousands of dollars on, planning for this day even when he'd lived in exile. He hadn't thought it possible that he'd ever be here, holding her still healing body while he tasted her ear. Smoke reveled that he could unsettle her with just one touch. One look. One little ring. But damn. She was killing him.

Sliding the ring out of its velvet crease, a big tear dripped down her nose and landed on the creamy plump swell of her breast. "I don't know what to say," she said as a hiccup choked out of her.

Smoke held his breath. It was so damned odd how a tiny little thing like Jess had always been able to stop him on his tracks. She'd just been through emergency surgery, and she'd survived an attack on her life, but she had to have known this day was coming. So why the slow roll? Was she still too weak? Was that all this was about?

Her head bowed. "Do you know what this means?" she asked, her voice small and too sad for Smoke's tough heart.

His body deflated. "I thought I did." Clearing his throat, he settled his back to the lavish pine headboard and tugged her along with him. "It means forever, Jess. To me it's just a ring, but on your finger, it means everything. It's the circle of our lives and our love. It's just you and me and this ranch and... what's the matter, darlin'?"

Jess turned carefully in his arms to face him. "It means I'm finally home, Smoke. I've... I've been alone for so long, but I deserted Ethan and you and..." She drew in a deep, shuddering breath, her voice rapping higher with every word. "I don't deserve to be this happy. He isn't even buried yet, and your mom and dad and..."

Oh, that. Smoke framed her face in both hands, his thumbs wiping the trail of tears from her flushed cheeks. This woman was sweaty and fragile, still dealing with too much loss. Yes, the funerals had been postponed until Smoke and Jess could both get on their feet, but reality was still damned tough.

Gathering Jess and that troublemaking ring into his arms, he pulled the sheet up to cover them both, and rocked her, his chin on the top of her head. "Stop beating yourself up, Jess. The funerals are only on hold until we're up to attending. An Ethan doesn't blame you. Hell, he was the one who pushed you to go to New York."

"Only because I nagged him."

"You know better. Ethan was as stubborn as you are, maybe more. If he hadn't wanted you to go, you wouldn't have gone. You would've been married to some short little jockey by now, barefoot and pregnant and dirt poor with three babies at your knees. Ethan only paid your way because he saw in you then what I see in you now. You're a star, Jess, and you always will be. You were made for better things than settling for less. Ethan wanted you to do something special with your life. He didn't want you stuck in a one-horse town. He wanted you to fly and fly high. Admit it, you know I'm right."

Lifting her index finger to her nose, she gave it a gentle swipe. "He *could* be a pain in the ass."

Smoke tilted forward and backward, more content that he could ever remember. "Ethan liked his beer, that's for sure."

"And football."

"And those stinking Cowboys." That was where Smoke drew the line.

Jess settled, the ruby still pinched between her fingers. "Would you put this on me?"

"Is that a yes?" He had to know.

"Yes," she said softly. "I will stand by you the rest of my life. I love you so hard."

Smoke snagged the piece of jewelry out of her fingers before he teared up along with Jess. He'd gotten damned sentimental lately. The ring was nothing compared to the priceless treasure sitting nearly in his lap, rubbing her naked butt against his manhood, and driving him out of his ever-loving mind.

She blew out a long sigh, her fingers outstretched, the pulse at the hollow of her neck throbbing. The ring fit perfectly, its star burning nearly as brightly as Jess's. "I love you to the moon and back," she whispered. "I hope you know that."

He tipped sideways, still holding onto her while he reached all the way over the edge of the bed pulled the next surprise, now wrapped in brown paper and tied off with baling twine, up off the floor. "This is for you, too."

Her brows arched as her eyes filled again. Smoke couldn't take any more female emotion, so he ripped the wrapping off and placed his gift in her hands.

"Oh my," she whispered breathlessly, her fingertips on her lips, and the silly secrets of a teenage boy revealed, his love for her then made known. "It's... it's beautiful."

"It's my heart, Jess." The heart he'd carved in that live oak when he was sixteen. The one she'd never known about. "It's always been yours. I carved it when you were just Ethan's bratty little sister. I knew it then." He gulped, his throat gone dry. "You're my soul. Hell, you're the best part of me."

With a tender groan, she set the carving to her side and twisted into him, still crying. Still glowing. Her lips mashed into his mouth, her tongue searching for entry. Hell, all she had to do was ask.

With a growl, Smoke gave Jess as good as he got, kissing the life back into her with every careful nip and tug, every lick of their tongues, and every pounding heartbeat between them.

The raging fire he'd kept tamped down these last few days, flared back to life, to Jess. As gently as he could, he rolled his bride-to-be onto her back. Then despite his own injuries, Smoke took careful advantage of her weakened condition. Before he was through, he'd anointed Jess's body up and down with his greedy tongue, kissed her out of her mind, and took her to the stars.

Matching him beat for beat and kiss for kiss, she strived against him. Clenching and pulling. Milking him dry. Leaving him sated and hopelessly head-over-heels in love. Finally spent, they collapsed in each other's sweaty arms, needing a break and maybe another nap before they molested each other again.

With her tucked neatly under his arm, Smoke stared at the ceiling, his body thrumming with the completeness of their mating. Jess was no dainty, fainting, feminine woman. She curled into his ribs, her fingertips light on his chest, rubbing her nose into the scruff on his cheek as she whined in that annoying I-want-an-ice-cream-cone-and-I-want-it-right- now way she'd always had. "I'm still hungry."

It was no wonder Ethan always gave in to her. "Give me a minute to catch my breath, woman," Smoke growled good-naturedly, patting her soft backside, now completely exposed with the sheets somewhere on the floor.

"I love it," she said as she stretched her left hand to admire her ring. "It's got a lot of fire in it."

Smoke slapped her ass gently, his long fingers grabbing as much of her posterior as he could. "That's why I bought it. It reminded me of you, all piss and vinegar."

Jess let out a low snort. "Wow, piss and vinegar, huh? You sure know how to tickle a girl's fancy."

He smacked her ass again, this time with a little sting. "I like tickling your fancy."

The revving engine of a motorcycle sounded outside their bedroom window. Jess leaned up onto one elbow, looking at the commotion. "Where's Colby going this early?"

"Home. To Boston. Her mother lives there." Smoke pressed a lingering kiss to Jess's cheek as he snuggled into his woman for the rest of his life. Her body tasted like warm caramel over vanilla cream with a hint of chocolate orange, his favorite food fest.

"I like her," Jess admitted, "but she seems lost, like she's looking for something."

"Nah, not Colby." Smoke smoothed his big hands over Jess's butt, massaging the sting of his last smack away. "She's not lost. She might've been before she joined the Army, but that woman knows exactly what she wants and where she's going. You'll see. The next time we hear from her, she'll probably have reupped."

Jess cuddled under his arm, her head on his chest as she let out a long sigh. "The weatherman said there's a storm coming. A tornado. We could lose everything."

Inhaling a long, cleansing breath, Smoke let his past go, along with all of its ghosts. "We'll be fine. There's a good-sized storm cellar out back. It's stocked with plenty of food and water, a couple beds. A radio and a generator. There's nothing to worry about."

She rubbed her cheek against his chest like a cat, purring and stretching her lithe body against his. "Is there enough room for the horses?"

Lifting his chin to the ceiling, he laughed at the notion of five horses and two mules in the storm cellar. He might just have to work out something for those four-legged kids of his, but damn. Finally.

Happily. Smoke had what he'd been searching for all these lost years. Room to breathe. A woman to love. A future filled with hard work, and the possibility of sons and daughters who would never know the sting of exile or the ache of betrayal.

He might have to come up with a new name for his ranch, though. Because *The Lost Chaparral* didn't feel so lost anymore.

And neither was he.

The End

Thank you for reading Smoke's story!

Be sure to check out the guys and gals from The TEAM in Irish Winters' series:
In the Company of Snipers

Other Irish Winters' books:

King of Hearts, Deuces Wild Series, #1
Joker Joker, Deuces Wild Series, #2
One-Eyed Jack, Deuces Wild Series, #3
Ash, Hearts and Ashes Series, #2
Angel, An SOBs Novel, #1

Coming soon

Assassin, An SOBs Novel, #2
Ace, Deuces Wild Series, #4

YOU ARE THE KEY TO THIS BOOK'S SUCCESS!

Please tell other readers why you like Smoke and Jessie's story by leaving an honest review at the retail site where you purchased it.

Recommend it to your friends. Lend it.

Most of all, enjoy it!

The best way to keep up with my new releases, giveaways, and actionable intel is to sign up for my spam-free newsletter at IrishWinters.com.

About the Author

Irish Winters

...is a best-selling author who, when she isn't writing, dabbles in poetry, grandchildren, and rarely—as in extremely rarely—the kitchen. More prone to be outdoors than in, she grew up the quintessential tomboy on a dairy farm in rural Wisconsin, spent her teenage years in the Pacific

Northwest, but calls the Wasatch Mountains of Northern Utah, home. For now. She believes in making every day count for something, and follows the wise admonition of her mother to, "Look out the window and see something!"

Connect with Irish online:

On Facebook:
https://www.facebook.com/author.irishwinters

On Twitter: https://twitter.com/irishwinters1

Or visit IrishWinters.com.